The Death of a Much-Travelled Woman

and Other Adventures with Cassandra Reilly

Also by Barbara Wilson

Cassandra Reilly mysteries

Gaudí Afternoon
Trouble in Transylvania

Pam Nielsen mysteries

Murder in the Collective
Sisters of the Road
The Dog Collar Murders

Other fiction

If You Had a Family
Cows and Horses
Miss Venezuela

Memoir

Blue Windows

The Death of a Much-Travelled Woman

and Other Adventures with Cassandra Reilly

by Barbara Wilson

 **Third Side Press**
Chicago

Printed on acid-free paper in the United States of America
Design and production by Midge Stocker

Acknowledgments

The following stories first appeared, with minor changes, in anthologies or
other media as noted:

"Belladonna" first appeared in *Women on the Case,* edited by Sara
Paretsky, Delacorte Press, 1996

"The Death of a Much-Travelled Woman" first appeared in
Womansleuth IV, edited by Irene Zahava, Crossing Press, 1991

"An Expatriate Death" first appeared in *Out for Blood,* edited by
Victoria Brownworth, Third Side Press, Chicago, 1995

"Murder at the International Feminist Book Fair" first appeared in
Reader, I Murdered Him, edited by Jen Green, The Women's Press,
London, 1989

"Mi Novelista" appeared in serialized form on *biztravel.com* in 1997

"The Theft of the Poet" first appeared in *A Woman's Eye,* edited by
Sara Paretsky, Delacorte Press, 1991

"Wie Bitte?" first appeared in *Brought to Book,* edited by Penny Smith,
The Women's Press, London, 1998

Library of Congress Cataloging-in-Publication Data

Wilson, Barbara, 1950–
    The death of a much-travelled woman : and other
adventures with Cassandra Reilly / by Barbara Wilson.
    — 1st ed.
        p.   cm.
    Contents: Introduction — The death of a much-travelled
woman — Murder at the International Feminist Book Fair — The
theft of the poet — Belladonna — An patriate death — Wie bitte?
— The last laugh — The Antikvariaat Sophie — Mi novelista.
    ISBN 1-879427-32-X (alk. paper)
    I. Title.
PS3573.I45678D43   1998
813'.54—dc21   98-30097
                                                              CIP

Third Side Press, 2250 W. Farragut, Chicago, IL 60625-1853
First edition, September 1998
10   9   8   7   6   5   4   3   2   1

for Jen Green

Contents

Introduction

Cassandra Reilly, translator, globetrotter, and accidental detective, came into being about ten years ago, on a train, appropriately enough, travelling through Norway. My companion Jen Green, an editor at the Women's Press in London, and I had just been at the International Feminist Book Fair in Oslo, and I was joking that the fair would be a great place to have a (fictional) murder take place. In 1986 I was still relatively new to the mystery genre and to the notion of what a feminist mystery might look like or what I might make of such a male-dominated tradition. I'd begun to experiment with *Murder in the Collective*, published two years before, and had just finished *Sisters of the Road*, which dealt with teen prostitution. Both were told in the voice of amateur sleuth Pam Nilsen, a printer and activist, rooted in her Seattle community.

"Would Pam solve the crime at the book fair then?" Jen asked.

"I can't imagine Pam ever leaving Seattle," I said. "No, it would have to be someone else, someone completely different."

Cassandra Reilly, who eventually did solve the book fair murder, *was* different. She wasn't rooted, she wasn't steadily employed, and her community was far-flung. To a large extent she reflected a shift that was taking place in my own life, a movement away from Seattle and into a wider world. In my early twenties, I'd lived abroad and travelled for

9

several years. In my mid-thirties, my work in publishing and translating, as well as a new transatlantic relationship, meant that I would be spending more and more time living away from Seattle and out of suitcases again.

Cassandra's life history did not come to me all in one piece. In fact, the first story in which she appeared, "Murder at the International Feminist Book Fair," revealed relatively few details about her. I never conceived her whole, as I had Pam Nilsen, a character so apparently realistic that I was frequently asked personal questions about her and her twin sister (personal questions I found, oddly enough, I could answer). Cassandra was less easy to pin down.

Some things I knew about her right away. She was a translator, from Spanish to English; that was a world I knew and an occupation that gave her a reason to travel. I based her in London, because that was where I was living off and on. I gave her an Irish grandfather, having had one myself. And I put her birthplace in Kalamazoo, Michigan, not far from where my mother was born and where she'd attended college. Most importantly, I gave Cassandra a craving to be in some other place from the place she was, a restlessness that was quite familiar to me.

But in most ways, Cassandra differed greatly from me. She was willingly expatriate—a choice I'd never been able to make—free-spirited, and of an eclectically amorous nature. She was tall and thin, much older than I (though by now I am almost caught up to her), and conveniently erudite. She seemed to know all kinds of things that I had to research and read books about. She spoke many languages well and had been to every part of the globe, several times. In bits and pieces over the years, she has revealed herself to me as not only adventurous and romantic, but also deeply melancholic and on the run from a past of deprivation and narrow-mindedness.

If Cassandra began to realize herself, mosaic-like, in my imagination, so did her circle of friends. One of them, her Australian pal Jacqueline Opal, I got to know quite well as Cassandra's sidekick in *Trouble in Transylvania*, but other friends were more reclusive. Her doctor friend Lucy Hernandez, for instance, with whom she always stays in Oakland, has only made one appearance, and the two women from whom she rents an attic room in Hampstead—Olivia Wulf, a refugee from Hitler's Austria, and Nicola Gibbons, a Scottish-born bassoonist—are glimpsed only tantalizingly in the background as yet. Gloria de los Angeles, the best-selling Venezuelan author whose novels Cassandra has translated, has never appeared in person either, but her rival, the Uruguayan Luisa Montiflores, has had a tendency to turn up right from the beginning.

Over the years, the mysteries Cassandra has investigated in foreign countries have enabled me to play with a variety of issues, some political, many literary. I've always chosen to interpret the mystery genre rather loosely. Frequently there is a murder; sometimes not. Puzzles of all kinds, robberies and impersonations, failed financial schemes, and hidden romances are quite as intriguing as dead bodies. After all, secrets are the heart of any mystery, and secrets take many forms. But the genre demands dead bodies, and dead bodies there are, along with suspects with bad alibis and relatives with suspicious motives.

As an amateur, Cassandra is drawn into all these situations out of coincidence and with the best intentions. Her work translating fiction has accustomed her to fluctuating meanings and alternative readings. As a translator, Cassandra is never in one world wholly; she shifts in and out of identities, cultures, even sexualities—for although in some urban subcultures of the West, being lesbian may be a fixed role, in other parts of the world there may well be more confusion, invisibility, and fluidity.

My interest in what could happen in the world of a translator-detective on the loose led me to write not only stories about her, but two novels. After I finished the second one, *Trouble in Transylvania*, I wondered if I would ever write another full-length Cassandra Reilly novel, because all the places I fantasized sending Cassandra (and friends have been very helpful, providing me a list of possible titles that range from *Chaos in Cambodia* to *Bonkers in Bolivia*) were as remote and intriguing as the Eastern Europe of *Transylvania*. I had spent some weeks travelling in Hungary and Romania, and many more weeks reading about the history and culture of those countries, in order to make the background of *Trouble in Transylvania* more convincing. Unfortunately my life and my other writing projects did not allow for extended visits to, much less extensive research about, Patagonia, Uzbekistan, and a matriarchal island off the coast of Okinawa—all places I was dying to set a mystery.

I contented myself with writing short stories instead, and with sending Cassandra to places with which I was more familiar. In the story form, I felt I'd found a medium that seemed to suit Cassandra Reilly's wayward nature and literary adventures. The mystery tale offers considerable pleasures. Not least is its ability to be read at one sitting. Brevity is the soul of wit, of course, but compression can also perform wonders with a plot. A single idea is all the story requires—no need for complicated subplots, no hordes of possible perpetrators, no nets-full of red herrings.

The first Cassandra stories were mostly written in response to requests from editors. Later I began to write them for their own sake, and for the pleasure of Cassandra's company. I'd found that as I travelled, I often ran into Cassandra Reilly in the most unexpected places. I'd see her at the Hamburg harbor, piloting a cabin cruiser up the Elbe River, and wonder what brought her there. Walking down a canal street in Amsterdam, I'd glimpse her again—tall, thin, with her wild hair clamped down by a beret—through the window of a used bookstore specializing in women's titles. I bumped into her at book fairs and on vacations to Hawaii and Mexico. I seemed to find her most often in London though, a city I'd left behind but she had not. Her connections there helped me remain connected too. And over the years, although I did not quite trust Cassandra to stay away from my girlfriends, she became a friend to me, a *compañera*. She gave me courage in difficult times and helped keep me amused during tedious hours on trains and buses. I listened to her stories, sympathized with the difficulties of trying to make a living as a translator, envied her zest for seeing the world, was fascinated by some of her friends and alarmed by her propensity for straying into situations where people seemed to be regularly murdered.

I am not Cassandra Reilly. I wouldn't exactly like to be Cassandra Reilly. But I enjoy being her companion, her amanuensis, her friend.

Other people in my life take an interest in Cassandra too and often suggest scenery for her to wander through and problems for her to solve. Few of their ideas have been ones I could use directly; still, a clipping that came from England in the mail, an anecdote told over dinner in Brussels, an environmental brochure from Germany—all became grist for the mill. The foreign flavor of these stories is no accident. I have spent years of my life outside the United States and have long-standing friendships and connections in many countries. In piecing together a portrait of Cassandra Reilly, expatriate dyke detective and open-eyed observer of what goes on around her, I've tried to give the sense of a life lived outside North America yet deeply American all the same— one of the essential themes of our New World literature, and one that crosses gender and genre.

The Death of a Much-Travelled Woman

It is a commonplace that in this world there are tourists and then there are travellers. Among the latter are the great travel writers, Jan Morris and M.F.K. Fisher, for example, who delight in words as much as famous sights and cities, and are inclined less to the rigors of the adventurous life than the luxuries or piquant poverties of foreignness. There are also the great travellers—Freya Stark, Gertrude Bell, Mary Kingsley, and Isabella Bird (a frail Victorian lady whose husband said of her, "She has the appetite of a tiger and the digestion of an ostrich.")—women who will, whatever age, seek out the bizarre and dangerous and coincidentally sometimes produce works of fine travel literature. And then there are the travellers, not very great, who write books, not very literary ones.

Edith "Tommy" Price was that last sort of traveller, that last sort of writer. And I'd adored her.

I'd grown up reading her books. My Aunt Eavan, who was something of a traveller herself, having ventured to Alaska before the cruise ships and Hawaii before the hordes, was a great fan of Tommy Price's and had collected all her books and sent copies on to me from the time I was eleven or twelve. *Jungle Journey, To the Top of the Very Top,* and *Lost in the Interior* were my favorites. For years they'd been out of print, but the British publisher Harridan had recently relaunched two volumes in a handsome new paperback edition, and interviews with Tommy Price had begun to appear in everything from the *Guardian's* Women's Page to *Spare Rib.*

She sounded such a dashing, risk-taking, literate woman that I determined to meet her. As an itinerant translator, I have travelled widely myself, but not always adventurously—at least not intentionally. My idea of foreign intrigue is an attractive woman at the next cafe table. I do admire my more intrepid sister voyagers, however, and have a nodding acquaintance with many. Therefore I wrote to Tommy Price at her home in Dartmoor and proposed a visit. I said I was in the process of translating her book, *Bound for Greenland,* into Spanish for an Argentinean publisher. This was not an entire falsehood. My dear friend Victoria, who runs a publishing house in Buenos Aires, *should* be publishing Tommy Price, and I'd have to make a note to persuade her one of these days.

A brief reply came immediately: "Tuesday, December 1, I shall be at home from three o'clock. Please join me for tea. Yours sincerely, Tommy Price."

I took the train to Exeter the morning of Tuesday, December 1, and then hired a car for the hour's journey to the small village of Sticklecombe-in-the-Moor. December was a bleak and glorious time of year to visit Dartmoor, and it was an appropriately bleak and glorious day, with wind sweeping over the yellow gorse and purple heather and sun breaking out dramatically behind the great rock piles, the granite formations called tors. It had been many years since I'd been in this part of the country; the last time had been with Sheila Cragworth, who was at the time nursing a desperate passion for a married woman and hoped to lose herself in the close study of geology and Neolithic archeological remains. I'm afraid I also learned perhaps more than I wanted to know about the way hot lava had once bubbled up to the surface where it cooled to become granite, and about the hut circles, barrows, monoliths, dolmens, menhirs, and kistvaens of the ancient people who once inhabited this severe landscape. It had been forested then; now it was bare and dramatic, with bogs and rivulets, granite rubble, and herds of Dartmoor ponies roaming freely through the military firing ranges.

Sticklecombe-in-the-Moor is an old market village hidden in a wooded valley by a river. It has a stone church, numerous tea shops, and at least one four-star pub for the walkers who throng to Dartmoor in the summer months. The address Tommy Price had given me was down a narrow lane with thick stone walls on either side. As I drove cautiously along, a wild rain burst out, and an oncoming car, in a great hurry, almost sideswiped my rented Ford Escort.

That was irritating, but not quite so irritating as arriving at Tommy's cottage to find no one at home. I stood on the step knocking loudly, wondering if she were deaf, or if she were the sort of woman who would deliberately invite a stranger to Dartmoor and leave her standing wretchedly in the rain outside. I remembered she had written in *Lost in the Interior:*

> At times, I know not why, a perversely asocial
> sensibility comes upon me, and I find myself doing and
> thinking things completely at odds with received
> notions of good behavior. It is precisely this
> misanthropic and contrary streak in my character
> which has enabled me to turn my back on civilization
> for months at a time and to embrace hardship and
> solitude with equanimity. Alas for my friends and
> family, however: the suddenness of my mood changes,
> the violence of my antisocial emotions!

Alas for Cassandra Reilly, standing on the step and becoming more and more soaked, the unwitting victim of a burst of antisocial contrariness!

Well, I could be contrary too. I returned to the car, found a bed and breakfast not far away, and changed my wet clothing. My landlady made me a cup of tea and commiserated about the failed visit to Tommy Price.

"She's not what you would call a friendly sort," Mrs. Droppington said. "Keeps to herself, she does."

"Has she lived here long?"

"Long enough. The cottage belonged to her brother, who retired here in the thirties. But he's been dead years and years now. Miss Price keeps the place up, I'll say that for her, but that's mainly the work of her friend, Miss Root."

"Miss Root?"

"Oh yes, childhood friend, I understand. Constance Root. She has always taken care of Miss Price's things while Miss Price was gallivanting around the world."

None of the books had ever mentioned a Constance Root.

"And is Miss Root a friendly sort?"

"The two of them keep to themselves mostly, but when Miss Price is away, I'd say Miss Root is friendlier."

I set out again for the Price-Root household about five, in the dark of an early evening thick with rain. Familiar country smells of animals and manure mingled with the acid scent of peat and bog from the hills above us. Sheila Cragworth had not believed any of the folktales and horror stories that abound in Dartmoor, about the Wisht Hounds and the ghosts and pixies, but I, granddaughter of Irish immigrants, couldn't help a shudder creeping back and forth across my shoulders, as I squished along the short road from Mrs. Droppington's. Dartmoor had been a place of great religious significance once, but all that was left were superstitions. I remembered reading that the only way to deal with pixies was to take off one's coat, turn it inside out, and put it on again.

It was too cold for that and so I only hurried on. This time I found a light on in the cottage window, a light that hadn't been there earlier.

I knocked. I knocked hard. And harder.

At length a gray head appeared in the window at the top of the door, and a low voice asked cautiously, "Who is it?"

"Cassandra Reilly. I had an appointment with Tommy Price for tea a few hours ago. But no one was here when I arrived, so I've come back."

The door slowly opened and a woman in her early eighties stood there in a plain dress with a heavy shawl over her shoulders and slippers on her feet. The stay-at-home, I thought: Miss Root who keeps the home fires burning while Miss Price is out writing books about her adventures.

"Please come in out of the rain," she said finally, when she could see I wasn't moving. "Miss Price isn't at home, I'm very sorry."

I stepped into the vestibule and couldn't help craning my neck for a view of a cozy-looking sitting room stuffed with books.

"She left very suddenly," the woman said.

I remembered the car that had almost sideswiped me in the narrow lane: Tommy Price on a sudden mission to Borneo perhaps.

"I can offer you some tea," Miss Root said. "I'm afraid I live very simply when Tommy is not here."

She invited me into the sitting room.

"Oh look," I said, going immediately to the bookshelves. "The original editions of *Out Beyond Outback* and *Kangaroo Cowboys*. I loved those books when I was a girl. I longed to go live in Australia."

A faint glimmer of pleasure drifted across Constance Root's wrinkled features, replaced almost immediately by one of disapproval. "Well, they're terribly outdated now. The modern day reality is surely quite different. I watch television and read the papers, and what Tommy described is not to be found in Australia today. I can't imagine why anyone would be interested in republishing such fairy tales."

"Oh, but that's part of the charm," I said. "We like to imagine a world where everything seemed simpler, where a traveller could come upon an enchanted place and describe it like a fairy tale. Nowadays it's all Hiltons and package tours."

Miss Root shook her head and went to put the kettle on for tea. I took the opportunity to scan the bookshelves for other favorite books. Tommy Price had a wonderful library of women's travel stories. Here were some of the classics: *Bedouin Tribes of the Euphrates* by Lady Anne Blunt; *My Journey to Lhasa* by Alexandra David-Neel; *Dust in the Lion's Paw,* the autobiography of Freya Stark; *A Lady's Life in the Rocky Mountains* by Isabella Bird.

Here too were hard-to-find, wonderful titles like *On Sledge and Horseback to Outcast Siberian Lepers* by Kate Marsden (1883); *To Lake Tanganika in a Bath-Chair* by Annie Hore (1896); and *Nine Thousand Miles in Eight Weeks: Being an Account of an Epic Journey by Motor-Car Through Eleven Countries and Two Continents* by Mildred Bruce (1927). Yes, and here were the complete works of Tommy Price, detailing her travels to Greenland, the Amazon, Tibet, Ethiopia, Australia—all written in the tough, no-nonsense prose that had so delighted me in my youth.

I opened *Kangaroo Cowboys* and read at random:

> It wasn't long before Jake guessed I was not the fearless British ex-soldier I had made myself out to be. "Why," he said to me one day as we were riding alongside each other through the bush, "you're a lady, ain't you?"

Miss Root came back in with a tea tray and I told her enthusiastically, "One of the things I really loved about Tommy Price was her disguises. Half the time she was masquerading as a man, but she also loved to get herself up in any kind of native costume. Do you remember how she disguised herself as a harem girl to get into the Sheik's inner sanctum?"

"Oh yes," said Constance dryly. "Tommy was quite the quick-change artist."

"I hadn't realized she was still travelling," I said. "Where's she off to this time?"

"The city of Pagan in Burma," Constance said. "She said she had an old friend there she wanted to see. At her age she's trying to pack in as much as possible."

The disapproving look came over Miss Root's wrinkled face again. I wondered how it must feel to be always left behind.

"You've known Miss Price a long time, I gather?" I said.

She shook her head and asked, "More tea?"

I returned to Mrs. Droppington's farm house and spent the evening curled up with *Kangaroo Cowboys*, which Constance Root had insisted I take.

"It can't make up for having come all the way from London, but please take it anyway. I know Tommy wouldn't mind."

The next morning I decided that I'd take a walk on the moors before returning to Exeter and London. I was disappointed not to have met Tommy Price, but felt inspired all the same. Would I still be on the go at eighty, visiting pagodas in the jungle? Or would I have retired to some quiet village like Sticklecombe-in-the-Moor? I had never been a true adventurer except in spirit; I liked a bittersweet espresso and a good newspaper far better than a jungle teeming with scorpions and snakes.

Mrs. Droppington fixed me a hearty country breakfast and warned me about straying too far from the paths.

"The mists and rain can come sudden up here. There's plenty of folks lost on Dartmoor every year."

I promised to be careful and took the Wellingtons and oilskin slicker she pressed on me, as well as a sandwich and thermos of tea for later. It was a clear morning, sunny and brisk, just right for walking, and I set off in good spirits, dutifully sticking right to the paths. The hills above Sticklecombe-in-the-Moor had a number of famous tors, those masses of bulging granite that look in some cases like great fists pushing their way up from the earth and in other cases like Easter Island gods, with enormous noses and full lips. To gaze out across the landscape was to feel in a very wild place, at the top of the world; yet the ground itself was hard going, being covered with what is called clitter, the rubble from outcrops of granite, and being squelchily wet. Dartmoor is poorly drained; the land is a like a sponge, with bogs among the tussocks of purple moor grass and tufts of whortleberries and wild thyme.

I walked for several hours, seeing few signs of life except for the occasional pony and, high above, the lark or stone curlew with its eerie cry. I had hoped to see some of the hut circles that Sheila Cragworth had been so keen on all those years ago, but all I saw were a few moorstones, the old stones along the ancient path that had been erected by villages like Sticklecombe-in-the-Moor centuries ago to help travellers find their way across the stretches of high ground. I remembered how irritating Sheila had found my superstitious bent. Poor old Sheila; she was now some sort of Tory functionary in Brighton, which showed what a broken heart could do to you.

I had lunch next to a particularly impressive tor that looked like a Northwest totem pole with a raven's beak and a bear's torso and finished *Kangaroo Cowboys:*

> Someone once said to me: Why travel? After all, there's nothing new to discover, no place where no one has been before. To that I would say that more than half of travel, perhaps ninety percent of travel, is imagination. Some people can stay home and live lives of great adventure; others may roam the entire globe and yet remain as provincial as a country lad. What you get out of travel is what you put into it; and if you put your whole imagination, you get a great deal.

I had difficulty reading the last words and raised my head to realize that, quite suddenly, the weather had changed.

An opaque white cloud was pouring over me like a sift of flour; but this cloud was wet and thick. It blanketed out the sun, the path, and even the tor at my back. Within a few minutes I couldn't see my boots in front of me. The fog quickly crept under my collar and through my clothes, until I felt chilled all over. I stood up, but had no idea which direction to move, or whether to chance moving anywhere.

Shapes and sounds were completely distorted; I thought I heard a curlew, and the cry made my skin crawl. The pixies were going to get me, if the Wisht Hounds didn't first. It was almost preferable to break my neck stumbling through the clitter, or to fall into a bog and drown. I hugged my arms to my chest and thought, 'be calm, the fog will lift in a minute.' But it didn't. It got worse. A howling wind tore at my hat, and pellets of hail whipped my face.

What would the intrepid Tommy Price do in a situation like this? Once, I remembered, she had run out of petrol in Greenland and had to walk for hours through a blazing white landscape without markers. She had kept her spirits up by singing Noel Coward tunes. I tried one in a quavering voice. In reality I wasn't much good with nature adventures. I was used to taking care of myself in awkward, unfamiliar, and even dangerous situations involving people, but weather was another matter. Weather was *serious*.

Still, thinking of Tommy Price helped a little. I flattened my body against the side of the tor and began to inch around its circumference. The cold granite scraped my face, but at last I found what I had vaguely recalled: a slit in the rock wide enough for a body to squeeze into. I don't know how long I sheltered there, but I had plenty of time to regret large portions of my life, particularly the portion that had begun the day before with my arrival in Sticklecombe-in-the-Moor. I assumed that if I stayed there long enough, a search party would be sent out for me. Possibly Mrs. Droppington, seeing the fog sweep over the moors, had already alerted the search-and-rescue mission.

I may have dozed a little; at least I thought I was dreaming when I sensed a lull in the wind and a slight thinning of the fog. It wasn't complete, but still, looking out from my crack in the tor I realized I could see boulders, and the path, and some furze bushes. That was enough for me; if I didn't get moving I would freeze to death—my fingers inside my gloves were already like ice. I charged down the path, hoping that by always going down I would find my way back to the valley. I couldn't see any markers, couldn't remember how many paths there had been. The landscape seemed completely changed; no longer did the moor seem a bracing plateau with bones of granite jutting up through the thin soil. It was a swampy morass of pea-green bogs and pools that I could only avoid sometimes by jumping from tussock to tussock.

Still, even if I was chilled to the marrow, haunted by the thought of vicious pixies, and terribly, hopelessly lost, the fog *was* lifting.

If it hadn't lifted, I doubt that I would have seen what I did: a tweed cap floating on a pool of green scum, and just underneath, the outlines of a woman's body, face down.

The coroner ruled the death of Tommy Price accidental. Everyone knew Miss Price's predilection for walking on the moors in every kind of weather. People did drown in the bogs—not often, but within memory. She was eighty-something, after all, and not as clear-headed as she could have been.

I returned to London with a violent cold and horrible memories of my headlong flight down the hill and into the first cottage I saw. The search party had no difficulty finding Tommy Price, in spite of my incoherent directions; apparently she had stumbled into a well-known bog, not deep but treacherous all the same. More than a few ponies had lost their footing there and tired themselves out trying to get free.

Even in London, I could not stop thinking about Tommy Price and Constance Root. Had it been Tommy who drove past me so quickly in the car? Why had Miss Root said Tommy was going to Burma when she was only out on the moors for a walk? That disapproval Miss Root had worn so plainly on her wrinkled face—was that envy? Or hatred? Perhaps she was jealous that Tommy Price's books were appearing in print again, that she was receiving public attention. But could she have been envious enough to kill Tommy? Would a woman in her eighties have the strength to push Tommy into a bog? And how would Constance have gotten Tommy up there in the first place?

Of course, the oddest thing was that when the constable came to Tommy Price's cottage to inform Miss Root of the sad news, she was not in. A note pinned to the back door canceled her milk delivery for an indefinite time. The car was gone.

"And she never came back," said Mrs. Droppington when I rang her a week later. "It's created an awful confusion here. You see, Miss Price left everything to Miss Root in her will, just like Miss Root left everything to Miss Price. Who's going to get it if Miss Root doesn't come back? I'm over there watering the plants every other day, but I can't do that forever."

I had a sudden image of Constance strolling among the golden pagodas of upper Burma. Could she have decided to do away with Tommy and to steal her plane ticket? The likeliest way for Tommy to enter Burma was to fly from London to Calcutta or Bangkok, then switch to a smaller plane and fly on to Rangoon. A few phone calls told me that a Miss Constance Root, not a Miss Edith Price, had booked a round-trip ticket with Air India to Calcutta on December 2, but that she hadn't used it.

That didn't mean that Miss Root hadn't murdered Tommy Price and taken quite a different flight. Perhaps Miss Root *had* been planning to flee to Burma after the murder and only my unlooked-for arrival had stopped her. However, for someone who had just murdered a woman and was preparing to escape to Burma, Miss Root had not seemed particularly agitated during my visit. Cold-bloodedness seemed much more likely to have been a characteristic of Tommy Price than of Constance Root.

I recalled a favorite passage from *To the Top of the Very Top:*

> James lay there, stiff as a corpse on a mortuary slab.
> "Frozen, poor old sod," I said to my companions.
> They were silent, struck with icy horror—James was the first of our party to die—who would be next?

25

"Well, don't just stand there," I said gruffly. "We'll never get him down the mountain. We'll have to bury him here, in the snow, on the side of Mount Ktchnqhtl. Yes, he'd like that, I know. James was a brave chap, a climber till the end."

Yes, it seemed far more plausible that Tommy Price, with her nerves of steel and her tough, resilient old body—hardened by years of trekking, sailing, and camel-riding—would be able to kill fragile Miss Root. But the motives for such a murder seemed even less clear. Why would Tommy, basking in the fame of rediscovery, decide to bump off her old companion, who perhaps had been her lover once, or least a good friend? Were there tensions between them that Tommy's sudden return to notoriety had inflamed? But if so, why didn't Tommy, with her vast acquaintance around the world, just leave? Why *didn't* she take that trip to Pagan?

I kept remembering the tweed cap floating on the green scum of the bog. After evading bandits and mercenaries and surviving frostbite and shipwrecks, what an inglorious end, to die face down in a pool of water.

It stuck me as curious that I couldn't remember ever seeing a photograph of Tommy Price. Not in any of her books, not in the interviews that had recently been published. I called an editor I knew at Harridan Press, which was reprinting Tommy's travel books, and asked Gillian if she had an author photograph.

"My dear," said Gillian. "I never even *met* Tommy Price. We corresponded by post and the odd phone call. She said her health was too bad to come to London, that she never travelled any more."

"What did her voice sound like?"

"Nothing special, rather low and pleasant, not particularly quavery, if you know what I mean."

That was Constance's voice all right; but it could also have been Tommy Price's.

"What's this all about, anyway?" asked Gillian.

"Oh, just curiosity. I was supposed to meet her, but it didn't work out. I'm sorry, that's all."

"Well I think she had a dashed good pop-off," said Gillian. "Terribly dramatic, don't you think, to sink like a stone into a bog on Dartmoor? We're changing the back cover copy on the next two reprints."

I went to the British Library and found all Tommy's books. Not a single one had a photograph inside or out, though there were plenty of drawings of Tommy in burnooses, chaps, and snow parkas with fur around the face. I couldn't help being struck, as I flipped through the different volumes, by how very many disguises she had assumed. Perhaps that's why she didn't want her photograph taken.

Or perhaps there was another reason.

I called Mrs. Droppington again.

"This might seem an odd question, Mrs. Droppington, but did you ever actually *see* Tommy Price?"

"Of course. What do you mean? That is, when she was at the cottage, which wasn't very often; that is, I suppose she was gone for stretches at a time; that is, I do remember seeing photographs of her as a girl when her brother lived in the cottage."

There was a lengthy pause, and then Mrs. Droppington said thoughtfully, "Do you know, my dear, you've set me thinking. It's a curious thing, but I am really not so sure after all that I did ever see Tommy Price all that much. Ever since Tommy took over the cottage and Constance came to stay, I suppose it's Constance I've seen. I knew from what Constance said that Tommy was often travelling. Constance would come into the greengrocers and say, 'Tommy's just back from Tanzania and says she absolutely must have sprouts for luncheon.'"

"But you couldn't exactly say what Tommy Price looked like?"

"I often saw her from a distance," said Mrs. Droppington. "Tommy loved to walk, you know. She was always striding across the moors, with her cap and walking stick. Quite a distinctive walk," Mrs. Droppington went on, gaining confidence. "Not at all like Miss Root's, which was so . . . feminine."

I had a theory, which might be hard to prove, that Constance Root and Tommy Price were the same woman. That Tommy Price, with her love of disguise, had invented a kind of alter ego in Miss Root. After all, the two of them hadn't moved to Sticklecombe-in-the-Moor until the 1970s, some years after Tommy Price's books had gone out of print.

I imagined Tommy to be a proud woman, one who would find it difficult to admit that because of age and money she could no longer travel so easily, nor, if she did, write about it in a way that anyone would find interesting. She didn't want to retire as Tommy Price and have people say that she used to be a famous traveller, so she came up with Constance Root, a proper English lady, who could live on very little, yet still, with her stories of Tommy Price's adventures, keep her past myth alive. When the books began to be reissued, Tommy Price must have been thrilled at first, and then increasingly worried that her secret would be revealed. Hence the ban on photographs. She didn't want anyone from the village seeing the face of Tommy Price in the newspaper and saying, "But isn't that our Miss Root from Sticklecombe-in-the-Moor?"

The strain must have been too much for her, so that she had decided to do away with herself. Which was why no one had seen Constance after Tommy's death and why the plane ticket hadn't been used.

Of course, such a theory had its soft spots. Why the camera-shy, reclusive Tommy had invited me to Dartmoor on the day before her suicide was the largest of them.

I travelled to Sticklecombe-in-the-Moor in the same way as before, by train to Exeter and then by hired car to the village. But this time I came very late at night. I parked my car in the village and, all in black, with only a flashlight, I walked quickly to the familiar cottage.

The wind whistled through the moonlit night. I tried not to think about Wisht Hounds and pixies. With tools I had borrowed from a friend in London whose East End family dabbled in the burglary trade, I let myself in the front door of the cottage.

It looked the same as it had two weeks ago when I had visited: the same old-fashioned furniture, dustier now, the same book-lined sitting room, illumined through the windows by moonlight. I went into the sitting room and let my flashlight play along the spines of all those wonderful old titles. Tommy Price hadn't been the only woman writing books in the 1930s. There had been Olive Chapman with *Across Lapland with Sledge and Reindeer;* and Rosita Forbes with *Unconducted Wanders and Adventures: Being a Gipsy Salad: Some Incidents, Excitements and Impressions of Twelve, Highly-Seasoned Years.* I wondered what had happened to those writers. I knew that sometimes a traveller only took one huge trip and then retired in triumph to dine off stories of savages or sultans forever—and that sometimes she kept going, year after year, like Freya Stark and Dervla Murphy, drawn to hardship and adventure long past the age when most women were settling down to crocheting and gardening. What a shame that Tommy Price hadn't had the courage to admit to her double life. She was never going to enjoy the acclaim now she so richly deserved. I couldn't help taking down the volume of *Bound for Greenland.* I had always loved its description of the end of the voyage. Softly I read aloud:

> I always considered myself a seaman of the first order, and it never occurred to me that my experience of the sea had been confined to tranquil oceans farther south, azure and emerald playgrounds for dolphins and humpback whales. This was a sea of ice floes as enormous as New York skyscrapers and vast swells the size of Himalayan mountains. Our ship had buckled and almost broken more than once; everything on the decks not tied down had been swept away and shards of glass and ceramic littered the galley where the

cupboards had been forced open. But now it was over, now the small band of us stood on the deck, on the mercifully horizontal deck, as Greenland, great Greenland, land of Eskimos and Vikings, land of ice mountains and majestic peoples, came into view. Thank God we were approaching land. At last.

"I always rather liked that passage myself," said a voice from the hall, a low pleasant voice, not at all quavery.

I was so stunned that I dropped the book and flashed my light every way but the right one.

"I wrote it, you know," the voice continued. "I wrote all those books. We thought it was a lark at first, Tommy and I. We would go to the British Library and look up information, or we'd talk to people who really had been to those places. Then we'd go back to our small flat in Bayswater and I'd use all my powers of imagination. It was a lark, but it also paid the bills. Times were hard then."

"So you've never been to any of these places?" I sat down in a lump on the sofa, hardly able to take it in.

Constance Root advanced into the sitting room and sat down opposite me. The moonlight gave the room an unearthly cast, but I could see her clearly. Her thin face was tired, yet I noticed she was wearing trousers and a heavy sweater and looked stronger than I remembered.

"We were poor as church mice. How could we travel?"

"Why did you use just Tommy's name?"

"My family was more respectable than Tommy's, you see. My father was a vicar in Somerset, and I had five brothers and sisters. They never would have let me go off to Australia on my own, much less Greenland. Tommy had just her brother, who retired from his job in Exeter to Sticklecombe-in-the-Moor. He was much older than Tommy and thought she was rather wild and boyish. It seemed perfectly plausible to him that his sister would spend all her time exploring foreign places."

I was still trying to take it in. "And your publishers? Didn't they ever check?"

"You must remember, my dear, that in those days there was no television and rather less general knowledge of what places looked like. Tommy found she loved acting the part of intrepid explorer, and our publishers loved it, too. Periodically she'd dress up in khaki and tall leather boots with a riding jacket and a tweed cap and swagger into the staid old office of Chatham and Son with a new manuscript. She refused to have her photograph in the books and, on my suggestion, said she always travelled incognito, in disguise. That was to prevent people in the countries we wrote about from realizing that she had never been there."

"But after the books were successful, didn't you have any desire to actually travel to foreign places?"

"Tommy did," said Constance. "But my thought was that neither of us would be able to take the kind of chances I took in the travel books, and that if by any chance we were exposed, it would mean the end of a rather lucrative career."

"I thought for a while that you and Tommy Price were the same person," I said slowly. "And that Tommy had created you as a kind of alter ego, someone to stay at home while she explored the world."

"You could just as easily say that I created Tommy Price as *my* alter ego," Constance said. "Someone to explore the world for me while I stayed home."

My eyes went to the shelves of books in their faded bindings. How many happy days I'd passed reading about Tommy Price's adventures. And now it turned out they were bogus.

"It must have been hard for you when the books began to be reprinted," I said. "And suddenly the world discovered Tommy Price again."

"Things had not gone so well with us in the last twenty years," Constance said, with lips pinched. "Sometimes it seemed as if Tommy had come to believe my stories about her. There were periods when she spent most of her time walking over the moors; and other times when she gave out that she was on a trip but stayed home and inside, expecting me to wait on her hand and foot. When the books began to be reprinted, at first I was happy, for it would be more income. But then I realized what it was going to be like living with her."

"Now you have the income, but no Tommy Price to worry you," I said. "I know she left everything to you in her will."

"Yes, she did."

"I'm curious about one thing," I said. "Why Tommy invited me here to visit."

"I didn't know she had until you turned up. It was rather unexpected, to say the least." Constance's wrinkled old face looked quite ghostly now, and evil, as if she were a Dartmoor pixie come back in human shape. No time to turn my jacket inside out now, either. "Perhaps Tommy had begun to be afraid of me and wanted a witness," Constance said, so cold-bloodedly that I couldn't help shivering. I remembered the toughness of her books. She hadn't hesitated to shoot imaginary tigers or draw her gun against rampaging kangaroos. Why would she stop at murder?

"And that ticket to Burma?"

"I bought it for myself, as a kind of reward, I suppose. I had always wanted to see the pagodas of Burma. But when I arrived at Heathrow on December second, I realized that such a trip was impossible for me. The years when I could have enjoyed it were long over. I passed two not very agreeable weeks at a bed and breakfast in Bournemouth and returned home earlier this evening. I'll spend the rest of my life here"—Constance's mouth twisted, ironically or cruelly, I couldn't tell—"answering fan mail for Tommy."

"And when did you push Tommy into the bog and hold her down? Was she drugged? Was the car that passed me that afternoon on the road your car, and were you driving her unconscious body to the moor and the bog? How did you manage it?"

"My dear Cassandra," Constance said distantly. "Tommy Price's death was accidental, as the coroner ruled. Everyone knows that Tommy loved the moors, and that the ground can be treacherously unstable. Why don't we just say that Tommy Price had the death she deserved: quick and dramatic."

"I think I had better tell someone," I said.

"No, you won't, my dear. You won't be believed, you know. Leave it as it is, and you'll be far more comfortable. You're only a tourist to the land of murder and I, after all this time, am now a traveller there."

Murder at the International Feminist Book Fair

"Dee!" I called to the woman in the pegboard exhibit stand, the small freckled woman with a round green cap who was staring a little woefully around her at unopened cardboard boxes.

"Cassandra Reilly, my girl!" She fell into my arms. "It's been years."

"Was it Manila or Auckland?"

"Manila," she said. "I missed Auckland. And now here we are at Vladivostok. Who could have imagined it?"

"Thank goodness for *glasnost*." I began to help her unpack the boxes. "Still just doing Canadian authors?"

"It's all you can get money for," she said. "Though of course as a loyal Canadian I'm convinced our writers *are* the best." She taped up a photograph of Serena Wood, Coastal Editions' star author. Back in the 1970s she had written a book on log cabin building for women, and it was still selling. "I thought they might be interested in this in Siberia," Dee said hopefully. "That's around here someplace isn't it?"

"Farther south, I think," I said, shivering slightly.

"How about you?" Dee asked. "Still doing Spanish translation? Still living in London? I don't know how you stand the place."

"Oh, it's all right," I said. "I'm hardly ever there, anyway. I just came back from six months in Latin America." I swung my briefcase for her to see. It was packed with manuscripts and books that I hoped to foist on reluctant publishers. "I'm on a translation panel tomorrow. One of my authors, Luisa Montiflores, is here. She's a depressed Uruguayan, very famous in some circles. Actually, I have to meet her now. Can we get together for lunch tomorrow?"

"Great."

The fair began with a flourish of speeches in Russian, English, with simultaneous translation into French, Spanish, Catalan, and Croatian. I looked around for a couple of hours and chatted with friends and acquaintances. Then I made my way over to Dee's stand, which now had, like all the others, a number and a sign printed by the Russian organizers. CAOSTAL EDITIONS. Well, it was close.

When I arrived, a tall woman in a black skirt, black leather jacket, black scarf, black boots, and black hat was haranguing Dee in an upperclass British accent.

"But my books do *extremely* well in England," she was saying. "My last novel was about a woman who left her husband for another woman, and it received *very* good reviews in the *Observer* and the *Times*." She pulled a clipping from her Filofax and read: 'Mrs. Horsey-Smythe treats this subject subtly and maturely, with none of the po-faced humorlessness characteristic of the so-called lesbian novel.' So, you see, there's no *reason* why it shouldn't do well in America. My agent doesn't understand why . . ."

"I'm sure your book is just wonderful," said Dee insincerely, "but, as I've been trying to tell you, I'm not an American publisher. Oh, Cassandra, hello!" She looked relieved to see me. "This is Felicity Horsey-Smythe. Cassandra Reilly. Cassandra lives in London too. Peckham or someplace, isn't it?"

Felicity gave me a smile the shape of a fingernail clipping and, pretending to see a dear friend across the hall, escaped.

"Don't say Peckham in public," I warned her. "Anyway, it was East Dulwich. But now I've moved. My bassoonist friend Nicola has offered me an attic room in the house she shares in Hampstead."

But Dee wasn't really listening. "Do you think I'm going to have to spend the rest of my life explaining to people that Canada is not a state of America? It even happened when the fair was held in Montreal. Felicity is fucking English— didn't she learn any geography?"

"Probably not in ballet school or wherever she went," I comforted Dee. "Can you leave your stand or should I get some food and bring it back?"

"Let's get out of here," she said. "The public doesn't come 'til two. I'm going to need all my strength to deal with the Rooskies."

"Has it been hard getting here?" I said. "These things are so easy for me. I just fly in and out."

"It gets harder every year to leave Vancouver," Dee said. "I'm not sure I'm cut out to be a jet-setting feminist."

"What? And miss out on all the gossip?" We went past the British women's presses, and I waved to a friend of mine at Sheba. "That's what these things are really about. Remember a few years ago?"

Dee's blue eyes began to sparkle. "The showdown between the Northern and Southern hemispherists?"

"Or Oslo?"

"It stayed light too late was the problem. It went to people's heads."

We laughed. "What about this year?" I asked. "Heard anything scandalous yet?"

Dee thought. "Well. You-know-who is here from Germany again . . . and . . . Oh, I know. Lulu Britten's got a stand."

"Lulu Britten?"

"The editor of *Trash Out*."

"Oh, really," I said. "That should provoke a few fireworks."

As an American expatriate, I was usually a little behind the times, but even I'd heard of the New York-based *Trash Out: A Journal for Contentious Feminists*. It was a forty-page monthly, stapled, on newsprint, with a glossy cover usually featuring someone in the women's community. Gloria, Rita Mae, Lily, Martina had been among the faces to appear on the cover. Inside was a lengthy (negative) assessment of their writing, performance, and lifestyle, spiced with innuendo and rude remarks from unnamed sources. CIA connections, drinking and drug bouts, hysterical displays of temper, peculiar sexual tastes, and, most of all, the hypocrisy of their moral public pronouncements contrasted with their sordid personal lives. It was hot and it was nasty. But that wasn't all.

In addition to the "profiles" of infamous feminists, *Trash Out* also offered blow-by-blow accounts of women's conferences rather in the manner of *off our backs*. The difference was that *Trash Out* rarely reported what went on during the panels and plenaries, instead giving the full treatment to cruel remarks and furious behind-the-scenes dissension. The journal also had a lengthy review section where critics slandered and dismissed feminist authors, musicians, and artists.

Feminism is in many ways a literary movement, so it wasn't surprising that *Trash Out* concentrated on well-known authors, nor that it had been able to exploit a market hungry for the low-down on mentors who had gotten too famous. The journal gave a voice to critics who were tired of being forced to at least appear to be giving a balanced assessment of writers' work and allowed the personal life of the writer to come in for as much dirt as possible. Yet the profiles, conference reports, and reviews were only part of *Trash Out*'s appeal. Many of its readers couldn't have cared less why such and such famous authors fell out, or why a certain author was no longer publishing with a certain press. What the average reader looked forward to every month was the letters section where any feminist could write and complain about her sisters.

Once we had "criticism/self-criticism," the Maoist-inspired exchange that used to come at the end of bruising political meetings. The "Trash Box" section of *Trash Out* was a little like that—but without the self-criticism. Women wrote in to detail the wrongs that had been done to them by ex-lovers, political enemies, feminist publishers, recording companies, theaters and galleries, and by their mothers and former best friends. In her editorials, Lulu justified this massive mud-slinging (and counter mud-slinging, because almost everybody wanted to reply) as "cathartic."

"For too long," she wrote, "we have been silenced by the false claims of sisterhood. We cannot live in the rarefied air of feminist solidarity. Our divisions are too deep to be mended, too harsh to be smoothed over. Only by speaking of our differences can we move forward . . ."

I said to Dee, "Do you think Lulu is here gathering dirt on the book fair for the journal?"

"No doubt. We'd better lie low," she laughed.

"Oh, we're too insignificant for her. She's never trashed anyone outside America, has she?"

"Margaret Atwood. Though possibly she thought she was American," said Dee. "Maybe I should sic her on Felicity Horsey-Smythe. After all, there is a certain prestige attached to being on the cover of *Trash Out*. It means you're important enough to criticize."

"It's funny, now that I think about it," I said. "Not only has the journal never had a non-American woman on the cover, it's never had a woman of color. Either Lulu has decided that women of color are out of bounds, or she's racist enough not to think they're important enough to trash."

"Maybe she's planning to remedy that. Look over there." Dee pointed across the central courtyard to where a couple of black women stood talking. Close enough to overhear, but not to be obvious, was a chunky white woman with glasses and a funny kind of topknot. She was swathed in as many scarves as a fortune teller, and her long, multicolored skirt reached her ankles. She was sucking on the tip of a pen and regarding the two women avidly.

"The woman on the right is Simone Jefferson," said Dee, "and Madame Zelda over there is Lulu."

"So you think Simone's her next victim?" It would make sense. With a brilliant first novel and a book of essays just out this year, Simone was already being compared to Alice Walker. She looked very young next to the older woman, a writer I recognized from Nigeria. "Do you think we should warn her?"

"Just a word maybe," said Dee. "Not that Lulu lets much of anything get in her way. She went to law school and knows the libel laws backward and forward."

The cafeteria was serving some kind of goulash. In front of us, a woman named Darcy Joanne from a feminist press in Santa Cruz, California was making a big deal about vegetarian food to the woman behind the counter.

"Macro-bi-otic," she repeated. "You know—tofu? Tempe? Nori? What about just some brown rice and broccoli?"

The thickset Russian woman stared at her and continued to hold out the goulash.

With a sigh Darcy took it. "Nobody thinks about the culinary aspects of where we hold these things," she complained to us. "God, remember Oslo? Twenty bucks for a seafood salad that turned out to be covered with artificial crab meat." Without a change in her voice, she went on, "These Russians. Have you met that poet Olga Stanislavkigyovitch or something? She's been pestering me all morning to publish a book of her poems."

"No," said Dee feelingly. "But I had some French deconstructionist yammering away at me for an hour about translating her book."

"Honestly," said Darcy, moving away to join a group from the States. "Everybody knows translations don't sell."

Later that day, after I'd spent an exhausting hour on the translation panel and an even more punishing hour in the company of Luisa Montiflores going over the reasons why her latest book had sold so badly in England, I stopped by Dee's stand to see how she was getting on. A very attractive young Russian woman was making her case to Dee.

"*Glasnost* is a farce. Everyone knows that. This fair is just another propaganda tactic. None of the real feminist or dissident writers are being allowed to participate. There is still repression, censorship, no possibility of emigration for dissidents or Jews. I say that in my poems and that is why my poems cannot be published here in the Soviet Union. They must be translated and published in English!"

"I can see your point," Dee said. "I really can. Really. But I'm only supposed to be publishing Canadian authors. I have enough trouble just publishing women. Oh look, here's Cassandra. She's a translator. Maybe she has some ideas."

I glared at Dee, but actually I did have some ideas—and some contacts in London and New York. After I'd written out a few addresses for Olga, I mentioned that she might want to keep a slightly lower profile. Just in case there were . . . you know . . .

"I am not afraid," said Olga. "I must say now what I think. It is my opportunity."

"Maybe she should go talk to Lulu if she wants publicity," said Dee. "She could write the first feminist letter trashing out the KGB."

"Who is this Lulu?" Olga demanded.

"Over there, but I was just . . . joking," she added, as Olga raced off. "Well, at least she's a good self-promoter."

The fair was by now packed with Soviet visitors, but there weren't many around Dee's stand. "They don't want to build log cabins?" I asked.

"I don't have enough lesbian books," Dee said glumly. "Look over there—Naiad Press is doing landslide business.

Beebo Brinker's never been on sale in the Soviet Union before."

"Is that what's causing the commotion?" I asked. "Is Ann Bannon making a personal appearance or what?"

"There's too many people to see," said Dee, straining. "But it doesn't seem to be coming from that direction."

The pushing grew stronger as people attempted to see what was happening, the muttering louder. Unfortunately, whatever message was being passed through the crowd was in Russian, so we were as much in the dark as ever. Suddenly we heard a siren outside, and then a phalanx of men and women in white rushed in with a stretcher. As the crowd parted, it was just possible, by standing on the chairs in Dee's stand, to see where they were headed.

Stand 103, the sign read. TRESH OOT. A few minutes later the stretcher went by again. And Olga was on it.

That night in the Vladivostok People's Hotel, Dee and I tried to make some sense of what had happened. According to Felicity Horsey-Smythe, who, with Lulu, was the nearest witness, Olga had been standing there talking to the editor of *Trash Out*. The next moment she had collapsed writhing to the floor and was dead within seconds. No one had seen anything untoward or threatening. There wasn't a mark on her. She'd simply gasped as if she couldn't breathe, clutched her throat, spasmed a few times, and gone down.

"And we laughed about the KGB," Dee moaned. "Did you see how fast those security men were on the scene? They got her out of there in no time. Oh yeah, they pretended to ask people what had happened, but that was just a ploy. They murdered her because she was a dissident!"

"Rubbish!" I said. "They'd be far more likely to arrest her and throw her in prison than to murder her in the middle of an international book fair. That sort of thing doesn't look very good."

But Dee refused to see that. "I think they should stop the book fair. I want to go home. It's too scary."

I ignored her wails. "Don't you think it's a strange coincidence that Olga keeled over right in front of Lulu's stand? It might make you think that . . ."

"Think what?" Dee was looking for bugging devices under the night table, in the closet. Soon her paranoia would have her taking the telephone apart, and turning up the radio while we talked.

"Let's get out of here," I said.

Felicity Horsey-Smythe was in a room down the corridor. When we knocked and entered, she was on the phone trying to get through to her agent in London. "That's Philip Fox-ton-ffoulkes," she was shouting to the operator, "ffoulkes, not Vooks. What do you mean he won't accept the charges?" She slammed down the receiver and said to us, "They're hopeless down there in reception. This is the eighth time I've tried to reach him today."

"Felicity," I said. "Do you remember what Olga was doing just before she died?"

"Oh, please, let's not go into that. I've spent the last two hours with a Russian detective, and my nerves are absolutely shattered. Olga wasn't doing anything. She was just standing there writing down something for Lulu, some address or something."

"Maybe Olga was trying to pass her a message and they had to kill her," suggested Dee.

"Nonsense," I said. A sudden memory of Lulu standing in the courtyard listening to Simone and sucking on her pen came back to me. I said casually, "So, whose pen was it anyway?"

"What do you mean? Well, Lulu's, I suppose. Yes, she picked up a pen lying on the stand table."

I tossed Felicity a pen from my pocket. "Could you just show me how Olga was standing, what she was doing?"

"Oh really," Felicity said. But she stood up and, holding the pen, she touched it thoughtfully to her mouth. "I told you, she was just standing there, thinking."

"Oh well," I said. "Thanks anyway." I nodded to Dee and we left.

Out in the corridor I could hardly contain my excitement. "That's it, don't you see?"

"What? Felicity said Olga wasn't doing anything."

"She *was* doing something. She touched the pen to her mouth, and the pen had poison on its tip."

"Oh my God." Dee leaned against the corridor wall. "Then Lulu poisoned Olga. But why? Is Lulu a KGB agent?"

I shook my head impatiently. "It's more likely that Lulu was the target. Someone knew about Lulu's habit of sucking her pens and substituted one with poison for an ordinary one. Olga was killed by mistake. The poison was really meant for Lulu!"

Dee stared at me. "Do you think we should tell her?"

"I think she may know. Did you see her face when they were taking Olga's body away?"

"But who could have wanted to kill Lulu?"

"That's the trouble. There are probably dozens."

"But only some of them are here at the fair."

Half an hour later we'd come up with a list of five names. Four of them had been featured on *Trash Out* covers in the past year. They were:

1. Jean Winthrup, a veterinarian who had written a popular book on lesbian sexuality and who had become a sort of sexual pundit/entertainer. An article in *Trash Out* had revealed that Jean's personal sexual habits weren't all that normal (she could only do it in a large kitty litter box) and had quoted a number of ex-lovers.

2. Monica Samson, a feminist poet who had won all sorts of major awards and who taught at Yale. *Trash Out* had exposed her work as unoriginal and accused her of plagiarism. The anonymous piece, possibly written by her rival Lois MacGuire, claimed that one of Monica's most famous books had whole lines lifted from an obscure Swedish woman poet of the nineteenth century.

3. Davis McKee, an influential feminist linguist/philosopher who had given lesbianism a whole new vocabulary of invented words. Detractors said she was like a kid who'd gone crazy with Pig Latin; admirers carried her dictionary around like the Bible. *Trash Out* had unleashed a scathing account of her financial holdings in South African companies.

4. Casey Walters, a prolific anthologist. For the past ten years, Casey had put together anthologies of poetry and prose on every conceivable subject that had to do with women. The *Trash Out* feature had parodied her by including "excerpts" from a supposed new anthology, *Feminist Chimpanzee Stories,* and its companion volume *Women and Parakeets: An Anthology.*

The fifth suspect, as yet unprofiled in *Trash Out,* was Simone Jefferson.

"I'd say she's the most likely," I said, "because she hasn't been trashed yet."

"But we don't know for sure that Lulu was planning to trash her," Dee said.

I looked at my watch. "It's only half past ten. Why don't we pay a visit to Lulu?"

There were voices in Lulu's room, but they stopped when we knocked. "Come in," said Lulu, a little unsteadily.

She and Felicity Horsey-Smythe were sitting rather close together on the single bed with glasses in their hands. A half-empty bottle of vodka stood on the night table beside them.

Dee and I perched on the armchair and declined to share the vodka.

Felicity said, "Lulu and I were just talking about what happened today."

"It was a real shock," Lulu said. She sounded pretty drunk. Her topknot was slightly askew, and her scarves twisted and jumbled around her neck. "Olga was a nice kid. She was going to write an article on Raisa Gorbachev for the next issue of *Trash Out.*"

"I told Lulu it would be more understandable if somebody had maybe been trying to kill *her*." Felicity laughed shrilly and took another gulp of vodka.

"Why do you say that?" I asked innocently. "To me it would seem just the opposite. If someone killed Lulu, it would mean they were probably on the cover of *Trash Out*. Then it would be purely a question of narrowing the suspects down. Why would anyone famous take a chance like that?"

"They probably would if they thought they could get away with it," Lulu muttered, pouring herself another drink. "I've had death threats, you know."

"Who here would you think most likely?" Dee asked. "I mean, if we pretended it was you, not Olga, who was the target."

A strange look passed over Lulu's face. "I've been wondering that myself. I have lots of enemies here."

"You should have thought about this when you started your journal," Felicity giggled. She'd taken off her hat, and her streaked blonde hair stood up wildly.

"I did think about it." Lulu's moroseness seemed to be growing in direct proportion to Felicity's vodka-induced gaiety. "But I wanted to go ahead. It was something I'd thought for a long time: investigating the fault lines in certain women's strength, exposing the pretensions and predilections behind the famous masks. A lot of people have said that wasn't fair, that these women didn't become famous on purpose, that it was their work that was important, not their personalities. I say that's garbage. No one becomes famous without wanting on some level to be famous. None of the women who've been on the cover is famous for her ideas alone. She's partly famous because she's got charisma or a beautiful face or because she's got ins with the right people or she's outrageous. She's famous precisely because she's a hypocrite, espousing one thing publicly, another privately, writing books or making speeches about feminism and sisterhood and screwing over any individual woman who stands in her way. To me that's not feminism, and women deserve to know what their heroines are really like."

"But what about Simone Jefferson?" Dee broke in, perhaps unwisely. "I've met her, and she's really nice."

"What about Simone?" Lulu said. "She's never been on the cover."

Felicity leapt in. "Well then, according to your theory, Cassandra, *she'd* be a good suspect, just because she wouldn't be suspected."

"She'd only be a good suspect if Lulu was planning to put her on the cover. But you're not, are you, Lulu?"

Lulu said nothing. She emptied her glass and stared very hard at the opposite wall. Finally she muttered, "I've got to get some sleep."

Dee and I stood up obediently. Felicity stayed right where she was.

"Well," said Dee, when we were back out in the corridor. "I thought Mrs. Horsey-Smythe was married."

"I'm sure she's just researching her next lesbian novel," I said comfortingly.

The next morning at breakfast we happened to stand behind Darcy Joanne again. She was asking for scrambled tofu and herb tea. "Well then, what about yogurt? What about all those Ukrainians who live to be 105 and only eat yogurt?"

Sighing, she took her plate of fried eggs and said, "Really incredible what happened yesterday, don't you think? I'm thinking of bringing out Olga's poems. They'd probably sell really well now."

"That's morbid," said Dee.

"That's publishing," Darcy replied. "You don't have to think about that stuff up in Canada. We do."

"Doesn't it seem odd that it happened in front of Lulu's stand?" I asked.

"Yeah," said Darcy. "If I didn't know better, I'd say Lulu had engineered it for publicity. She's in real financial trouble—that's the rumor. I don't know how she could afford to come here."

"But I thought *Trash Out* was a huge success."

"It had novelty value," Darcy said. "But that's worn off. People are saying that it sounds the same every month. And nobody but feminists are interested in the dirt on other feminists. But Lulu put a lot of money into it. I guess her loans are probably coming due. Cash-flow problems—that's the polite term for imminent bankruptcy." And Darcy drifted off to join her Californian friends.

"Yeah, I know she has me in mind for her cover," said Simone, almost in resignation. We'd caught up with her in the courtyard outside the exhibit hall. "But what can you do? Better Lulu trashing me out than Ishmael Reed. At least Lulu doesn't pretend to be the voice of injured black manhood."

"But what can she dig up on you?" Dee asked. I wanted to warn her that this was a potential murderer we were dealing with, but Dee rushed on, "I *love* your work. And your life has seemed so straightforward. I mean, at least in that article I read in *Time* magazine. You went to college, graduate school, and then published a novel."

Simone smiled. "Nobody's life is that straightforward. Everybody does little deals, makes little trade-offs, has skeletons in the closet. Mine are no worse than anybody else's, but I have them. For instance, I'm a lesbian, but I'm not out to a lot of people, and I don't write about lesbian characters. That's how I want it at the moment; that's how I can do my best work at the moment. But Lulu's bound to make that the focus. I'm angry, but I'm prepared."

Simone's face was a calm mask. I couldn't really tell what she was feeling and thinking.

"It's terrible about Olga, isn't it?" I said.

But Simone just nodded.

"Either Simone's a liar or we've got the wrong suspect. And she didn't look upset about Olga at all."

Dee and I were back at her stand, surrounded by hordes of Russians. If anything, Olga's death had increased the attendance at the book fair, and there was an especially large crowd around TRESH OOT.

"Maybe we should give up," said Dee. "The Soviets probably killed Olga. And if they didn't they'll have to figure out who did."

"Rubbish," I said. "What does the KGB know about feminism? They have no idea it's a greater threat to world stability than capitalism. No, there must be a connection somewhere—to the idea that Simone is somehow involved and the rumor that Lulu's losing money on *Trash Out*."

Fifteen minutes later I had broken into Lulu's room at the Vladivostok People's Hotel. I realized how little I knew about her as I leafed through a box of back issues of *Trash Out* and rooted in a suitcase full of scarves and black underwear. There must be a clue here somewhere, but I was damned if I knew what it was or where to find it.

I heard footsteps in the corridor and hastily crawled under the bed. While I held my breath, the footsteps continued down the hall and disappeared. I scrambled out again. But my eye had been caught by a crumpled piece of paper in between the bed and the night stand. It looked as if it had been thrown there in a fit of anger. I smoothed it out and read:

POISON PEN

Some authors are sensitive about their secrets. I found that out the hard way during the most recent international feminist book fair in Vladivostok when Simone Jefferson tried to poison me with a quantity of strychnine placed on the tip of my pen. Like many people, Simone had noticed that I'm in the habit of sucking my pen when I'm thinking. So she substituted one that had poison in order to shut me up. The only reason I'm here today is that there was only enough of the substance to make me really ill, not enough to kill me. Otherwise I would have been murdered in cold blood in the very midst of the book fair, while selling this journal.

Lulu went on to detail the means by which Simone was caught. The bottle of rat poison in her hotel room. Her fingerprints on the pen. "All because," Lulu wrote, "Simone was afraid I was going to finally expose the secret she'd hidden for so long. Her lesbianism."

Again I heard footsteps in the corridor, but this time I wasn't fast enough. I was on my hands and knees by the bed when Lulu came in. She immediately spotted the paper in my hand.

"I didn't mean to kill Olga," she said, edging toward me while she kept the door well blocked. "Nobody can accuse me of premeditated murder. That editorial is proof. The poison was meant for me. That's not a crime, is it?"

"No," I said. "Not if you really meant to commit suicide. But you miscalculated the dose; you only thought you'd get ill and that Simone would be blamed. It was a big risk to take, Lulu. And Olga took the consequences."

I couldn't see any way around her body to the door.

"No one's going to know," she said, coming closer to me. "I've still got some strychnine here and, as we both know, it doesn't take much."

"I've always thought," I said calmly, "that all those scarves were a big fashion mistake." I grabbed the ends of one of them and started twisting.

The door behind her burst open.

"KGB!" said Felicity Horsey-Smythe playfully, and then gasped. "Oh my, Cassandra dear, whatever are you doing to poor Lulu? She looks as if she can't breathe very well like that."

"Be a good girl, Felicity," I said, still keeping a firm grip on Lulu, "and call the police, dear."

A half hour later Simone had retrieved the bottle of rat poison Lulu had planted in her room, and we'd presented it together with Lulu's editorial to the Soviet police. I had no idea what would happen to Lulu now; whether she'd be tried and punished, sent to Siberia, or locked up in the Lubyanka. Whatever her punishment, I suspected it would be milder than what some of Lulu's victims would have meted out if they'd had the chance.

Still, I suppose some good did come out of it all. Felicity Horsey-Smythe had a wonderful subject for her next novel, and Darcy Joanne said she'd publish it in the States. They signed a contract at the Vladivostok Airport and agreed to move quickly on the project. They did want, after all, to get the book out in time for the next international feminist book fair.

"Tierra del Fuego!" said Dee when I told her. "I can hardly wait."

Theft of the Poet

It started gradually. Here and there on London streets new blue plaques that might have been placed there by the authorities, if the authorities had been reasonably literate and unreasonably feminist, began to appear. At 22 Hyde Park Gate, the enamel plaque stating that Leslie Stephen, the noted biographer, had lived here was joined by a new metal plate, much the same size and much the same color, which informed the passerby that this was where writer Virginia Woolf and painter Vanessa Bell had spent their childhoods. Over in Primrose Hill, the plaque noting that Yeats had once been resident in this house was joined by a shiny new medallion gravely informing us that Sylvia Plath had written the poems in *Ariel* here before committing suicide in 1963.

Above the blue plaque at 106 Hallam Street, the birthplace of Dante Gabriel Rossetti, another one appeared to emphasize that poet Christina Rossetti had lived here as well. The plate at 20 Maresfield Gardens, which recorded that Sigmund Freud had passed the last year of his life here, was joined by a new one telling us that Anna Freud had passed forty-two years at this address. A medallion to Jane Carlyle, letter writer, joined that of her famous husband Thomas at 24 Cheyne Row, and a plaque telling us about Fanny Burney, author of *Evelina* and other novels, appeared above that describing Sir Isaac Newton's dates and accomplishments on the outside of a library in St. Martin's Street.

The appearance of these blue plaques was at first noted sympathetically, if condescendingly, by the liberal newspapers, and a certain brave editor at *The Guardian* was bold enough to suggest that it was high time more women writers who had clearly achieved "a certain stature" be recognized. The editor thus managed to give tacit approval to the choice of authors awarded blue plaques and to suggest that the perpetrators had gone quite far enough. "We wouldn't want blue plaques on every house in London, after all."

But the plaquing continued, heedless of *The Guardian's* pointed admonition, to the growing excitement of many and the consternation of quite a few. Who was responsible and how long would it go on? Would the authorities leave the plaques up or bother to remove them? Apparently they had been manufactured out of a lighter metal than the original plaques, but instead of being bolted to some of the buildings, they had been affixed with Super Glue. Some residents of the buildings were delighted; other inhabitants, in a conservative rage, defaced the medallions immediately.

The next blue plaques to go up were placed on houses previously unrecognized as having been the homes of women worth remembering and honoring. A plaque appeared outside the house in Maida Vale where authors Winifred Holtby and Vera Brittain had shared a flat for several years. A similar plaque commemorating the relationship of poets H.D. and Bryher appeared in Knightsbridge. Mary Seacole, a Victorian black woman who had travelled widely as a businesswoman, gold prospector, and nurse in the Crimean War and who had written an autobiography about her life, was honored on the wall of 26 Upper George Street off Portman Square, as was Constance Markievicz, many times imprisoned Irish Republican, who was the first woman elected as a member of the British Parliament (though she refused to take her seat in protest over the Irish situation), and who was born in Westminister on Buckingham Street. Of course, my friends in the progressive backwater of East Dulwich were delighted when Louise Michel, the French Revolutionary Socialist and Communard, was honored with a plaque, and those of us who are interested in printing and publishing were quite thrilled when a plaque appeared at 9 Great Coram Street, home in the 1860s to Victoria Printers, which Emily Faithfull set up in order to train women as printers and where she published Britain's first feminist periodical.

The list could go on and on, and it did. You would have thought the authorities would be pleased. Tourists flocked to obscure neighborhoods; guidebooks to the new sites proliferated; tours were organized; handwritten notes appeared on walls suggesting plaques; letters to the editor demanded to know why certain women hadn't been honored. Other letters criticized the manner in which only bourgeois individuals were elevated and suggested monuments to large historical events, such as Epping Forest, where Boadicea, the leader of the Celts, fought her last battle with the Romans in A.D. 62, or the Parliament Street Post Office, where Emily Wilding Davison set fire to a letter box in 1911, the first suffragist attempt at arson to draw attention to the struggle for women's rights. One enterprising and radical artist even sent the newspapers a sketch for a "Monument of Glass" to be placed on a busy shopping street in Knightsbridge, to commemorate the day of March 4, 1912, when a hundred suffragists walked down the street, smashing every plate glass window they passed.

The Tory and gutter papers were naturally appalled by such ideas and called for Thatcher (whom no one had thought to plaquate) to put a stop to the desecration of London buildings and streets. Vigilant foot patrols were called for and severe penalties for vandalization were demanded.

This then was the atmosphere in which the news suddenly surfaced that the grave of a famous woman poet had been opened and her bones had gone missing.

As it happened, the small village in Dorset where the poet had been buried was also the home of a friend of mine, Andrea Addlepoot, once a writer of very successful feminist mysteries, back when feminist mysteries had been popular, and now an obsessive gardener and letter writer. It was she who first described the theft to me in detail, the theft that the London papers had hysterically headlined: POET'S GRAVE VANDALIZED.

My dear Cassandra,

By now you have no doubt heard that Francine Crofts "Putter" is no longer resting eternally in the small churchyard opposite my humble country cottage. My first thought, heretically, was that I would not miss the hordes of visitors, primarily women, primarily Young American Women, who had made the pilgrimage to her grave since her death. I would not miss how they trampled over my tender flowers, nor pelted me with questions. As if I had known the woman. As if anyone in the village had known the woman.

And yet it is still quite shocking, and everyone here is in an uproar over it.

You of course realize that the theft is not an isolated action, but only the latest in a series of "terrorist acts" (I quote Peter Putter, the late poet's husband) perpetrated on the grave, and most likely not totally unrelated to the unchecked rememorializing of London and surrounding areas. (Discreet plaquing is one thing, but I really could not condone the defacing of Jane Austen's grave in Winchester Cathedral. Surely, "In Memory of Jane Austen, youngest daughter of the late Reverend George Austen, formerly Rector of Steventon," says everything necessary. There was no reason on earth to stencil onto the stone the words "Author of *Pride and Prejudice* and other novels.")

These "terrorist acts" consisted of the last name, "Putter," in raised lead lettering, being three times chipped off from the headstone. The headstone was repaired twice, but the third time Mr. Putter removed the headstone indefinitely from the grave site. That was over a year ago and it has not been re-erected, which, despite what you might think, has not made my life any easier. I cannot count the number of times that sincere young women have approached me as I stood pruning my roses and beseeched me, most often in flat American accents, to show them the unmarked grave of Francine Crofts.

Never Francine Putter or Francine Crofts Putter.

For Francine Crofts *was* her name, you know, even if at one time she had been rather pathetically eager to be married to the upcoming young writer Peter Putter and had put aside her own poetry to type his manuscripts. Francine Crofts is the name the world knows her by. And, of course, that's what Putter cannot stand.

I know him, you must realize. Although his boyhood was long, long over by the time I moved here (after the enormous financial success, you recall, of *Murder at Greenham Common*), his parents Margery and Andrew and sister Jane Fitzwater—the widow who runs the local tearoom, and who has a penchant for telling anyone who will listen what a shrew Francine was and what a saint dear Peter—still live in the large house down the road that Peter bought for them. This little village represents roots for Peter, and sometimes you'll see him with one or another young girlfriend down at the pub getting pissed. When he's really in his cups, he'll sometimes go all weepy, telling everyone what a raw deal he's getting from the world about Francine. It wasn't his fault she died. He really did love her. She wasn't planning to get a divorce. They were soul mates.

It's enough to make you vomit. Everybody knows what a cad he was, how it was his desertion of her that inspired Francine's greatest poetry and the realization that he wasn't coming back that led to her death. It's hard to see now what she saw in Putter, but, after all, he was younger then, and so was she. So were we all.

But Cassandra, I'm rambling. You know all this, I'm sure, and I'm equally sure you take as large an interest in the disappearance of Francine's bones as I do. Why not think about paying me a visit for a few days? Bring your translating work, I'll cook you marvelous meals,

Barbara Wilson

and together we'll see—for old times' sake—whether we can get to the bottom of this.

When I arrived at Andrea's cottage by car the next day, she was out in her front garden chatting with journalists. As usual she was wearing jeans and tall boots and a hat that suggested hunting big game rather than deadheading spent roses. At the moment she was busy giving quotes to the journos in her usual deep, measured tones:

"Peter Putter is an insecure, insignificant man and writer who has never produced anything of literary value himself, and could not stand the idea that his wife was a genius. He drove her to . . . Oh, hello, Cassandra." She broke off and took my bag, waving good-bye to the newspaper hacks. "And don't forget it's AddlePOOT—not PATE, author of numerous thrillers. . . . Come in, come in." She opened the low front door and stooped to show me in. "Oh, the media rats. We love to hate them."

I suspected that Andrea loved them more than she hated them. It was only since her career had slipped that she'd begun to speak of them in disparaging terms. During the years when the feminist thriller had been in fashion, Andrea's name had shone brighter than anyone's. "If Jane Austen were alive today and writing detective stories, she would be named Andrea Adlepoot," one reviewer had gushed. All of her early books—*Murder at Greenham Common, Murder at the Small Feminist Press, Murder at the Anti-Apartheid Demonstration*—had topped the *City Limits* Alternative Best Seller list, and she was regularly interviewed on television and in print about the exciting new phenomenon of the feminist detective.

Alas, any new phenomenon is likely to become an old phenomenon soon and thus no phenomenon at all. It never occurred to Andrea that the feminist detective was a bit of a fad and that, like all fads in a consumer culture, its shelf life was limited. Oh, Andrea and her detective, London PI Philippa Fanthorpe, had tried. They had taken on new social topics—the animal rights movement, the leaky nuclear plants on the Irish Sea—but the reviews were no longer so

58

positive. Too "rhetorical," too "issue-oriented," too "strident," the critics wrote wearily. The fact that Andrea couldn't write a sex scene to save her life led to a further decline in sales at a time when women's erotica filled the bookstores, and Andrea retired for good to Dorset.

"Cassandra, it's shocking how this is being reported," she announced as we sat down in the tiny parlor. She took off her safari hat and her gray curls bristled. "Peter Putter is here giving interviews to the BBC news every few hours. And now the Americans have gotten wind of it. CNN is here and I've heard that Diane Sawyer is arriving tomorrow."

"Well, Francine Crofts was born in America," I said. "And that's where a lot of her papers are, aren't they?"

"Yes, everything that Putter couldn't get his hands on is there."

"I read somewhere that he destroyed her last journal and the manuscript of a novel she was working on."

"Oh, yes, it's true. He couldn't stand the idea of anything bad about himself coming to the public's attention."

"Any chance he could have removed the bones himself?" I asked.

Andrea nodded. "Oh, I would say there's a very good chance indeed. All this rowing over her headstone has not been good publicity for our Peter Putter. It puts him in a bad light, keeps bringing back the old allegations that he was responsible in great measure for Francine's death. It's quite possible, I think, that he began to read about the appearance of all these new blue plaques and thought to himself, 'Right. I'll get rid of the grave entirely, blame it on the radical feminists, and there'll be an end to it.' I'm sure he's sorry he ever thought to bury the body here in the first place and to put 'Putter' at the end of her name. But he can't back down now, so the only solution was to arrange for the bones to disappear."

"I don't suppose we could go over to the graveyard and have a look?"

Andrea peered out her small-paned front window. "We'll go when it's quieter. Let's have our tea first."

We had our tea, lavish with Devonshire cream and fresh scones, and then Andrea went off for a brief lie-down and I, left to my own resources in the parlor, went to the bookcase and found the volume of Crofts's most celebrated poems.

They struck me with the same power as they had when I had read them twenty years before, especially the poems written at the very end—when, translucent from rage and hunger, Francine had struck out repeatedly at the ties that bound her to this earth and that man. Even as she was starving herself to death in the most barbaric and self-punishing way, she still could write like an avenging angel.

Around five, when the autumn mists had drifted down over the small village in the valley, Andrea roused herself and we walked across the road to the tiny churchyard of St. Stephen's. The small church was from the thirteenth century and no longer in use; its front door was chained and padlocked. The churchyard was desolate as well, under the purple twilight sky, and covered with leaves damp from rain. It was enclosed on all sides by a low stone wall and shielded by enormous oaks. We went in through the creaking gate. The ground was trampled with footprints, and many of the graves were untended.

I could barely see my feet in front of me through the cold, wet mist, but Andrea led the way unerringly to a roped-off hole. There had been no effort to cover the grave back over, and dirt had been heaped hastily by its side.

It had the effect of eerie loneliness and ruthless desecration, and even Andrea, creator of the cool-headed Philippa Fanthorpe, seemed disturbed.

"You can see they didn't have much time," she murmured.

Suddenly we heard a noise. It was the gate creaking. Without a word Andrea pulled me away from the grave and around the side of the church. Someone was approaching the site of the theft, a woman with a scarf, heavy coat, and

Wellington boots. She stood silently by the open grave a moment. And then we heard her begin to cry.

Ten minutes later we were warming ourselves in the local pub, The King's Head. A few journos were there, soaking up the local color—the color in this case being the golden yellow of lager. Andrea bought me a half of bitter and herself a pint of ale, and we seated ourselves in a corner by the fireplace. The woman in the churchyard had left as quickly as she had come. We were debating who she could be when the door to the pub opened and a paunchy man in his fifties came in, wearing a tweed jacket and carrying a walking stick.

"That's how he dresses in the country," Andrea muttered. "Sodding old fart."

It was Putter, I assumed, and I had to admit that there was a certain cragginess to his face that must have once been appealing. If I had been a lonely American working at a publishing house as a secretary in the early 1960s, perhaps I, too, would have been flattered if Chatup and Windows's rising male author had shown an interest in *me* and asked *me* if I'd like to do a spot of typing for him. Putter's first novel, *The Man in the Looking Glass,* had been published to enormous acclaim, and he was working on his second. An authentic working-class writer (his father was actually a bank clerk, but he kept that quiet)—who would have guessed that this voice of the masses would eventually degenerate into a very minor novelist known mostly for his ascerbic reviews of other people's work in the *Sunday Telegraph*? Poor Francine. When she was deserted by her young husband, with just one book of poetry published to very little acclaim at all, she had no idea that within two years their roles would have completely reversed. Peter Putter would in the years to come be most famous for having been Francine Crofts's husband.

"I wish it were possible to have a certain sympathy for him," Andrea said gruffly, downing the last of her ale. "After all, we both know what it is to experience the fickleness of public attention."

I went up to the bar to order us another round and heard Putter explaining loudly to the journos, "It's an outrage. Her married name was Francine Putter and that's how I planned to have the stone engraved in the first place. I only added Crofts because I knew what she had brought off in that name, and I wished in some small way to honor it. But the radical feminists aren't satisfied. Oh, no. It didn't satisfy them to vandalize the headstone over and over; they had to actually violate a sanctified grave and steal Francine's remains. No regard for me or her family, no regard for the church, no regard for her memory. God only knows what they plan to use her bones for. One shudders to think. Goddess rituals or some sort of black magic."

"You're suggesting a Satanic cult got hold of Francine?" a journo asked, and I could see the story in the *Daily Mail* already.

"Wouldn't surprise me in the least," Putter said, and he bought a round for all the newspapermen.

I returned to Andrea. "If you were a radical feminist and/or Satanic cultist, how would you have stolen the bones?"

She glowered at Putter. "It was probably dead easy. Drive over from London in a minivan, or even a car with a large boot. Maybe two of you. In the hours before dawn. One keeps watch and the other digs. The wooden casket has disintegrated in twenty years. You carefully lay the bones in a sheet—so they don't rattle around too much—wrap the whole thing up in a plastic bag, and Bob's your uncle!"

I shuddered. Blue plaques were one thing, but grave robbery and bone-snatching, even in the cause of justified historical revisionism, were quite another.

"Why not just another gravestone, this time with the words Francine Crofts?"

"Do you really think Putter"—Andrea shot him a vicious look—"would allow such a stone to stand? No, I'm sure whoever did it plans to rebury her."

"What makes you think that?" I asked. "Maybe they'll just chip off pieces of bone and sell them at American women's studies conferences."

"Don't be medieval," Andrea said absently. "No, I think it's likely they might choose a site on the farm not far from here where Francine and Peter lived during the early days of their marriage. The poems from that period are the lyrical ones, the happy ones. A simple monument on the top of a hill: Francine Crofts, Poet." Andrea looked up from her pint and turned to me in excitement. "That's it. We'll stake the farm out; we'll be the first to discover the monument. Maybe we'll catch them in the act of putting it up."

"What good would that do?"

"Don't be daft," she admonished me. "It's publicity, isn't it?"

Andrea wanted to rush right over to the farm, but when we came outside the pub the fog was so thick and close that we decided to settle in for the night instead. I went to up the guest room under the eaves with a hot-water bottle and Crofts's *Collected Poems*. I'd forgotten she had been happy until Andrea reminded me. Her memory was so profoundly imbued with her manner of dying and with her violent despair that it was hard to think of her as celebrating life and love. But here were poems about marriage, about the farm, about animals and flowers. It made one pause: if she had married a faithful and loving man, perhaps her poetry would have stayed cheerful and light. Perhaps Putter did make her what she was, a poet of genius; perhaps it was right that he still claimed her by name. But no—here were the last poems in that first collection, the ones that had been called pre-feminist, protofeminist, and even Ur-feminist. Some critics now argued that if only Francine had lived to see the women's movement, her anger would have had a context; she wouldn't have turned her fury at being abandoned against herself and seen herself a failure. But other critics argued that it was clear from certain poems, even early ones, that Francine understood her predicament quite well and was constantly searching for ways out. And they quoted the poem about Mary Anning, the early nineteenth-century fossil collector who was the first to discover the remains of an ichthyosaurus in Lyme Regis, not far from here, in 1811. It was called "Freeing the Bones."

The next morning Andrea and I drove over to the farm and skirted the hedges around it looking for a spot that the unknown gravediggers might decide was suitable for a memorial of some sort.

"This is such a long shot," I said. "But isn't it quite possible that some Americans were involved and that they've taken the remains back to America? Wasn't she from Iowa? They'll bury them in Cedar Rapids."

"Francine would hate that if she knew," said Andrea. "She was such an Anglophile that she couldn't wait to get out of Cedar Rapids. It was the pinnacle of happiness for her to study at Oxford and then to get a job here afterward. No one, not even her family, tried to make a case for sending her bones back to Iowa."

The farm was owned by an absentee landlord; it was solitary and lovely on this mid-autumn day. We broke through a weak hedge and tramped the land, settling on one or two likely little rises where the monument might go. Francine's spirit seemed all about us that afternoon, or perhaps it was just because I'd been reading her poetry. It would be nice if she were reburied out here in the open, rather than in that dank little closed-in churchyard. I imagined picnics and poetry readings under the oak trees. With bowls of food left on the grave to feed her starved soul.

Late in the afternoon we returned to the village and decided to have tea in Francine's sister-in-law's tea shop. It had occurred to me that perhaps it had been Jane Fitzwater crying at Francine's grave last night.

The Cozy Cup Tea Shop was packed with journalists, however, and one look at Jane was enough to convince me that it had not been she in the dowdy coat and Wellingtons. Jane, a bit younger than her brother, was less craggy but still imposing, with bleached blond hair and a strong jaw that gave her the look of a female impersonator. Her dress was royal blue and so was her eye shadow—coordinated, no doubt, for the cameras.

She barely gave Andrea and me a second glance when we entered but consigned us to an out-of-the-way table and a waitress who looked to be only about twelve and who brought us very weak tea, stale scones, and whipped cream instead of clotted cream.

"*Whipped* cream?" said Andrea severely to the little waitress, who hunched her shoulders and scurried away.

Jane Fitzwater had seated herself at a table of journalists and was holding forth in quite loud tones on the absolutely undeserved amount of publicity that Francine had gotten through her death. "I say, if you're unhappy, take a course in weaving or a holiday abroad. Don't stew in your own self-pity. And I tried to tell Francine that. All marriages go through difficult times, but Peter would have come back to her eventually. Men will be men. Instead she had to hide away in that little flat of hers and stop eating. Oh, I tried to talk to her, I even brought her a casserole one day—I could see she'd gotten thinner—but it never occurred to me, and I'm sure it never occurred to Peter, that she was deliberately trying to starve herself to death. And then he gets all the blame. It's made a broken man of him, you know. Never recovered from the shock of it, he hasn't. Ruined his career, his life. She should have thought of that when she did it, but no, always thinking of herself, that's how she was right from the beginning. My mum and dad noticed it right off. 'Seems a little full of herself,' my dad said the first time Peter brought her to Dorset. 'Talks too much.' My mum felt sorry for her, of course. Francine didn't have a clue about life, really, her head was in the clouds. 'It will end in tears,' my mum said. And she was right."

"I've got to get out of here," Andrea muttered to me. "Or it will end in something redder than tears."

We left the tea shop and strolled through the village, which was scattered with posh cars and vans emblazoned with the logos of television stations, native and foreign. Peter Putter was over in the churchyard giving an interview to what appeared to be a German film crew.

"It's enough to make one lose one's appetite entirely," Andrea said and slammed the door to her little cottage.

That night I was awakened from a deep sleep by the sound of a car driving down the road to the village. Normally it would not have been anything to wake up to, but I had a sudden odd feeling that it was the car I'd borrowed to come here. I staggered over to the little garret window, but saw nothing. I crept down the steep stairs and peeked into Andrea's room.

She was not there.

I went out the back door and saw that the small Ford was gone.

Since Andrea didn't have a car, I supposed she'd taken mine. Perhaps she'd decided to visit the farm by herself to stake out the gravediggers; perhaps she'd heard someone else's car driving down the road and decided to follow it. Whatever my suppositions, my actions were limited. The farm was a good four miles away, it was raining, and—I finally looked at the clock—four in the morning. I got dressed just to keep warm and paced around a bit, then remembered that Andrea had a bicycle out in the shed behind the cottage. With the feeling that there was nothing else to do, I steeled myself for cold and rain and set off into the dark night.

With water streaming down my face, I pedaled furiously, wondering why roads that always seemed to be perfectly flat when you drove over them by car suddenly developed hills and valleys when you were travelling by bicycle. Still the cold rain gave me an incentive for speed, and I arrived at the farm in record time. There were no cars at the side road leading to the farmhouse, so I got off the bike and began to reconnoiter on foot around the hedges. There must be another road leading to the farm, but I would waste more time looking for it than going on foot.

By this time my clothes were soaked and my boots caked with mud. I tried to retrace the steps Andrea and I had taken the day before, but in the darkness it was hard to see the difference between land and sky, much less between a rise and fall in the earth. Then, through the hedges, I saw a small light. I broke through and started staggering over the land toward it. It was joined by another small light.

The lights seemed to be dancing together, or were they struggling? One of the lights vanished. I began to hear voices. Had Andrea discovered the perpetrators; was she fighting with them?

But then I heard a voice I thought I recognized. "Put those bones down! I'll have you in court for this. Grave robbing is a criminal offense as well as a sin!"

"What you did to Francine is a sin and a crime," another even more familiar voice shot back. "Give me back my shovel. She deserves to have a better resting place than the one you gave her."

"I was her husband, I have a right to decide where she's buried."

"You gave up your rights long ago."

Then there was only the sound of grunts as they grappled again.

"Peter," I said. "Andrea. Stop this. Stop this right now!"

I picked up one of the flashlights and shone it at each of their faces in turn. "What's going on here?"

"I suspected her right from the beginning," said Peter, looking like a large wet muskrat in his brown oilskin jacket. "I've been keeping an eye on her. Lives right across from the churchyard; easy enough to break into the grave. Tonight I heard the car starting up and decided to follow her. Called the journalists first, they'll be here in a minute. You'll go to jail for this, Addlepoot!"

"Oh, Cassandra," groaned Andrea. "I'm sorry. I had it planned so differently."

But she didn't have time to exonerate herself. The journalists were suddenly on us like a pack of hounds; there were bright lights everywhere, illuminating a stone marker that said FRANCINE CROFTS, POET and a muddy sheet piled, haphazardly, with thin white bones.

Some weeks after this, when I was back in London, Andrea came up to see me. If it hadn't been for the surprising intercession of Mrs. Putter, Peter's mother (for she had been the woman we'd seen crying at the grave), Andrea would have been on trial now. As it was, Francine's bones were back in the churchyard of St. Stephen's, and Andrea had closed up her cottage and was thinking of moving back to London.

"I didn't have completely ignoble motives," she said. "I always did believe that Francine deserved better than a Putterized headstone or no headstone in a grim little grave under the eye of people who had hated her. But I have to admit that I saw an opportunity. When the blue plaques started to appear, I thought, why not? Someone's bound to do it, why not me? I wouldn't say I was the one who'd done it, of course. I'd steal the bones, rebury them, erect a marker and then—with you as a witness—I'd discover the new site and let the media know. It would have been the best kind of publicity, for me *and* for Francine. I would have solved a mystery, my name would be back in the news, my publisher might decide to reissue my books, . . . but instead . . ."

"Instead the newspapers called you a grave robber and filled the pages of the tabloids with photos that made you look like a refugee from *Nightmare on Elm Street*. And they spelled your name wrong."

Andrea shuddered. "I'm going to have to put all this behind me. Start over. Science fiction perhaps. Or why not feminist horror? Skeletons that walk in the night, the ghosts of Mary Wollstonecraft and Emily Brontë that haunt us still today . . ."

"I did read in the newspaper today," I interrupted, "that the owner of the farm has decided to put up a marker to Francine himself, and to open the farm up to readings and poetry workshops. Apparently he's something of an artist himself, in addition to being a stockbroker. He said he never knew that Francine had lived there. So something good came of it."

Andrea cheered up. "And Putter didn't look so terribly fabulous in those photographs either."

We started to laugh, embarrassed at first, and then with gasping and teary amusement, recalling our wet night in the mud.

Then we went out for a walk to look at some of the blue plaques that had gone up recently. For, you see, the remembering and honoring hadn't stopped.

There were now more blue plaques to women than ever.

Belladonna

I.

It is over a year since I spent the day with you on your lovely island. I remember it all very vividly . . .

—Georgia O'Keefe,
letter to her hosts on Maui

For a long time I turned up my nose at Hawaii. The very name reeked of junior-high talent shows where pimpled hula dancers tried to keep their cellophane skirts up and their flowery wreaths from falling into their eyes. Luaus with barbecued pigs, tiny paper umbrellas decorating tall, lethally sweet cocktails, muscular tanned youths with surfboards, Waikiki, Gidget, Magnum P.I.—those are the images that came to mind when people said, "You've never been to Hawaii? You've never been to Hawaii, and you've been to Patagonia and the Ivory Coast?"

But that's the point. We who call ourselves travellers are snobs of the worst kind. We would much prefer to be wildly uncomfortable on the cushionless seats of a bus in Bangladesh or a train traversing the Gobi Desert, moving slowly through some strange desolate landscape and either feeling boiling hot or freezing cold, with nothing to eat, no toilet paper, and nothing to read, surrounded by hostile people who don't speak our language and perhaps want to convert

71

us to their religion or to steal all our money, than to do anything so *gauche* as to enjoy ourselves in any sort of tropical paradise, particularly if it means that another Westerner, a mere tourist, might be anywhere in sight.

Luisa Montiflores, the gloomy and recondite Uruguayan novelist, was not of the same opinion. She had just spent three "cold like hell" winter months as a writer-in-residence at the University of Toronto and wanted to recuperate on the Hawaiian islands. And she wanted me, as her translator, "my *friend*," to join her.

Luisa had once been my protégé, but over the years, the situation had reversed itself. I had been a lone voice championing her difficult, deconstructionist novels, sending sample translations of her work to publishers and writing articles that proclaimed her originality. Now I had lost interest in her work, just as academics and the literary elite were discovering her peculiar blend of poetry and self-pity. Although I suspected that hardly a thousand people in the English-speaking world could have read her work, Luisa attracted honors, grants, stipends, symposia, and residencies all over the world.

"All, all I owe to you," she often said. "I am loyal, you see," and to prove it she frequently stipulated that a translator's salary be part of her agreements. From Stockholm to Adelaide we had travelled the globe together, and if it had truly been my goal in life to be Luisa's literary factotum, I'd have been ecstatic.

We had just been to the University of Hawaii in Honolulu where Luisa gave a seminar talk on the new Latin American fiction, which was, strangely enough, only about her fiction. Now we were in Maui, where Luisa planned to stay a month to put the final touches on her latest novel, and talk to me about translating it. We were staying with Claudie, a friend of Luisa's who was an art dealer in Lahaina.

"When Gloria de los Angeles goes to give a talk, they do not ask her about *my* work. Why do they ask me about *her*?"

Luisa glared at me. "I still do not understand, Cassandra, how you can also translate her. That idiot and her magic realism. I spit on her magic realism."

"You're writing for different audiences," I soothed her. "Believe me, your work and hers cannot even be discussed in the same breath. Do you think the most brilliant minds of Spanish language departments are impressed by her writing? I can tell you, Luisa: they laugh at her. Simply laugh at her and shrug their shoulders. But when they say Luisa Monti-flores, they bow their heads in respect."

We were sitting on a terrace overlooking Claudie's mag-nificent garden of ginger, hibiscus, and trailing orchids in the warm, sweet-scented evening. I had managed to keep up my anti-tropical-paradise attitude through this morning's arri-val at the Honolulu airport, with its refrigerated leis and prêt-à-porter pineapples. But by the time the day was over, I was half-converted, and by the time our plane had taken us through an indigo and passion fruit sunset to Maui an hour ago, I was babbling like an idiot. "Just look at that surf! And look, palm trees swaying in the wind!"

Luisa looked slightly mollified; she stroked the white streak in her sleeked-back dark hair. As usual she managed, in her Oxford shirt and loose slacks, to appear both careless about her clothes and impossibly elegant. I attributed it to the good posture she'd acquired at her Swiss boarding school.

"Everyone is reading Gloria de los Angeles," she said, but with a slight smile now. "Every airport I am in, I see her books. Pah! She is a fool. She is *over-accessible,* a tramp."

Claudie laughed, "Oh Luisa, always the same worries!" Claudie was wearing a silk print shirt in tangerine and lemon over a pair of crisp white shorts and sandals. Her skin was a warm desert-sand tone—Filipina, I guessed—and her straight black hair swung all in one piece like a curtain. I had just been in St. Petersburg; coming from a bitter winter, my black Levi's, cowboy boots, and worn bomber jacket felt completely inappropriate for the lush warm breeze. Under-neath my beret, my crazed graying hair frizzed out humidly.

Like Claudie's, it was all of a piece, but more a piece of untended topiary than a swaying curtain of black light.

Luisa took a long drink of iced tea and shrugged off poor, pathetic, over-read Gloria. "Claudie," she said abruptly, remembering something. "Where is your Nell? The last time I was here, you had your Nell."

Claudie's smile was almost easy. "Oh, Nell and I have broken up. She goes her way. I go mine."

"But the gallery?"

"She kept it. I got the house. Some of the artists went with Nell, some with me. I'm hoping to get another storefront."

"But Claudie, this is not good. What happened? No, I know what happened! Another woman, no? I'm killing her."

Claudie laughed. "Oh Luisa, you're always the same. It's too late. It happened six months ago. One of those things. Believe me, it wasn't easy for any of the three of us. No one's to blame. I could have been the one to leave too."

"That's different, if *you* leave," said Luisa firmly. "That's passion. Otherwise, it's just betrayal."

"I'm getting used to being single," Claudie began, on a positive note, and then the telephone rang and she excused herself.

When she was gone, Luisa announced, "That Nell was no good anyway. You know the type: restless, a toughie, a big mouth, always feeling sorry for herself. You know I can't stand that. Claudie is my friend from Paris; we went to cinematography school together. She deserves a good woman. Perhaps you're interested, Cassandra?" Luisa eyed me speculatively. "When are you settling down?"

"When are you?"

"Me? Every day I don't commit suicide is a miracle." But Luisa was laughing now. "My writing is my only mistress. When you see what I have written, you will be amazed and astounded. It is the best work I have ever done, no kidding."

"The most extraordinary thing," Claudie said, returning with more iced tea and sitting down. "That was a woman on the phone named Donna Hazlitt, calling from the Hana coast, on the other side of the island. I don't know what to make of it, whether she's lucid or completely confused. She was talking about a small painting that she said she discovered among her dead husband's things. He apparently inherited it from his parents. It's unsigned and seems not to have been quite finished, but Mrs. Hazlitt seems to think it might be an O'Keefe. Mrs. Hazlitt is interested in having it appraised and in selling it. She wants me to handle the sale for her."

"O'Keefe? You mean *Georgia* O'Keefe?"

"The very same. She came here, you know, in the Thirties, courtesy of Dole Pineapple. They hired her to do two paintings for advertising purposes. They set her up on the Big Island, but when she asked if she could live among the workers on the plantation, the Dole people said absolutely not. She never did end up painting any pineapples for them while she was here. Eventually, in desperation, they air freighted a pineapple to her in New York and she managed to paint it, very unenthusiastically."

Claudie put down her iced tea without drinking it and stood up again. "The critics were never very excited about O'Keefe's Hawaiian paintings, but I think some of them are lovely. There was an exhibit two years ago at the Honolulu Academy of Arts—it caused quite a stir. Gorgeous flowers, of course—crab's claw ginger, hibiscus, plumeria, lotus, and jimson weed—which she called *belladonna*—those lovely angel's trumpet weeds. There were also some landscapes from Maui. She stayed here for a few weeks, escaping the Dole people. Waterfalls and mountains in the Io Valley, and black lava on the Hana coastline."

Claudie paced up and down the terrace. "I can't tell if Mrs. Hazlitt is on the up and up. She just started talking in the middle, as if we'd been discussing this for years. She said it's a flower, an angel's trumpet. Oh, what a coup if this is for real. It would make all the difference to me. Mrs. Hazlitt wants me to drive out there tomorrow to look at it. Why don't the two of you come?"

In a shop in Lahaina, where we stopped the next morning to buy a few provisions, I saw a T-shirt proclaiming, "I survived the Hana Highway."

All too soon I knew what that meant. The Hana Highway was a two-lane road that twisted around the north coast of the island like dental floss around teeth. The landscape was spectacular all right: a dark cobalt sea and only slightly lighter sky, waterfalls at every other turn and black lava rock formations and black sand beaches. Claudie's Toyota, however, was a compact, and although Claudie and Luisa, being small and fined-boned, fit quite well, I had some trouble with my long legs.

And with my stomach, which insisted on lurching in rhythm with the car.

Luisa wanted to know more about O'Keefe, and Claudie had obliged by giving her a life history, ending with "She was essentially a solitary woman. Even though she was married to Steiglitz, she still managed to live her own life and spent half the year in New Mexico. I never really think of her as having been married at all."

"Have you ever noticed," I asked, "how much we admire heterosexual women who remained single or *as if* single? Simone de Beauvoir, Gloria Steinem, Maya Angelou. With lesbians, though, it's a different story. We don't want to discount their relationships; we *want* them to be coupled."

"I am never coupled," said Luisa. "I couldn't ask anyone to share my suffering." As always when she talked about her depressions, she began to laugh hugely.

"I think you're right, Cassandra," said Claudie. "Is it perhaps because lesbians are not supposed to have the problem of being misunderstood and held back by their mates?"

"Or because being a lesbian rests so much on proof. You need to actually have a lover by your side before you're believed."

"I know that part is true," sighed Claudie. "Since Nell left me, a few people—relatives mostly—have asked if I'm seeing any nice men."

"I am opposed to marriage for creative people," said Luisa. "An artist's life is always solitary. You two, on the other hand, are not artists, only the hand-maidens to creativity. There is nothing to prevent you getting together with each other. Why don't you?"

In the embarrassed silence that followed, Luisa murmured, "Claudie, pay attention to your curves, please."

Around the small town of Hana were a luxurious resort and clusters of houses on the hillsides. We pulled up a driveway half-hidden by ferns and hibiscus bushes to a simple but beautifully constructed wooden house, low and long.

Claudie knocked on the door, but there was no answer.

"That's odd," she said, looking again at her scrap of paper. "We're right on time and this is the right address."

We waited for half an hour on the steps, drove away to the resort for a cool drink, and then came back. There was still no sign of Donna Hazlitt.

"I hate to have come all the way out here for nothing," Claudie said, and sounded close to tears. "I guess she changed her mind. Maybe she decided to take the painting to a gallery in Honolulu."

I'd had the feeling there was something odd about this adventure from the beginning. As the afternoon shadows lengthened, the impression grew stronger. I began to walk around the house, looking for a window I could at least peer into. Most of them were tight with blinds. Finally, in the back, I was able to peer through an opening in the blinds into what appeared to be a bedroom.

The closet was open and clothes were strewn about; the drawers had been treated the same way. And on the floor near the bed lay the still body of an elderly woman in a dressing gown, a still body that did not move when I called out, and would not move again.

The next day back in Lahaina, the news was all over the local paper. Donna Hazlitt, long-time resident of Hana, had apparently been the victim of a robbery-murder. But subsequent editions of the paper backed down: there were no signs of breaking and entering, and nothing of value had been taken, though Hazlitt, the widow of a coin and stamp collector, had many obvious things to steal.

It also appeared that what appeared to be murder may have really been a case of accidental poisoning. Apparently Mrs. Hazlitt had recently been treated at the local clinic for uvevitis, an inflammation of the iris, for which she'd been prescribed atropine. The atropine came in a small dark brown bottle with a glass dropper and was similar to a second brown bottle found next to it on the kitchen counter. This second bottle held echinacea in a tincture of alcohol and was a herbal remedy for strengthening the immune system. The echinacea was usually taken orally, in a glass of water. Authorities speculated—and then, and after tests, concluded—that Mrs. Hazlitt had mistaken the two bottles. Instead of putting drops of echinacea into her glass of water before she went to bed that night, she'd poured atropine in instead. Taken internally, atropine is a poison that attacks the nervous system and causes flushed skin and a terrible thirstiness. If untreated, the symptoms increase to a state of delirium, in which the victim makes spasmodic movements and then falls into unconsciousness and death. The amount of atropine in the glass shouldn't have been enough to kill her, but Mrs. Hazlitt was almost eighty and had a heart condition. She'd certainly shown all the signs of poisoning, including evidence of the spasmodic movements in the disorder in her room.

Donna Hazlitt was known to be a solitary, rather mousy, and inoffensive woman, who had inherited her house and money from her husband. They had no children and she had no enemies. The coroner gave a verdict of accidental death by alkaloid poisoning.

Of course, there was no mention, in the papers or anywhere else, of a Georgia O'Keefe painting.

II.

Everyone has many associations with a flower—the idea of flowers. You put out your hand to touch the flower—lean forward to smell it—maybe touch it with your lips almost without thinking—or give it to someone to please them.

—Georgia O'Keefe

About a week after our trip to Hana, I took a stroll through downtown Lahaina one morning. It had been an old whaling village, and a few structures remained from that period. There were a few lovely wooden arcades and a big old house where the Christian missionaries had lived, recording their astonishment at the ways of the Hawaiians, who seemed to enjoy singing and dancing, especially unclothed, as often as possible.

As usual I was pondering not only the multiple ways of interpreting Luisa's texts, but the problem of Luisa herself. In our typical fashion, we'd followed a pattern of glad reacquaintance, instantly followed by impatience on my part and a wounded sensibility ("You don't understand me!") on hers. This morning she'd accused me of willful language distortion and vowed to find another translator, someone who would appreciate her as the great genius of twentieth century literature. "Good," I'd snapped. "And good luck finding someone who will put up with your megalomania, too!"

I stopped now outside a gallery window to look at some flower paintings. Many of the galleries in Lahaina catered to tourists of the lowest common denominator and featured canvases of unbelievable awfulness, which depicted mystical underwater scenes—dolphins frolicking amidst schools of parrotfish and Moorish Idols, with the submerged towers of Atlantis in the background.

But the watercolors displayed in this window were different: small, modest, exquisite. There was hibiscus the color of coral and rose, lying on a yellow tablecloth; a ginger plant with the cobalt sea in the background; and finally, the single petal of a plumeria flower, unfurling off the page, softly shirred at the edges, dark at the center, leading you into its heart. I thought, if these aren't too expensive, perhaps I'll buy one for Claudie. She had been so shaken by the whole experience with Donna Hazlitt that she had hardly come out of her room for days. She had told the police several times about the phone call, but it was clear they were not planning to take her information into much account.

I stepped inside the door of the gallery, and immediately a woman came forward from between two of the small paintings. She was in her thirties, with a smooth bronze tan and soft, lingering brown eyes. Her hair was sun-bleached past blond to something closer to a light lemon cream. Her teeth were startlingly white when she spoke, in a deeper voice than I'd been expecting, but a voice that fit with how she looked, attractively roughened by the elements.

"Can I help you?"

I told her I might be interested in buying one of the paintings.

"Great!" she said, and couldn't help beaming like a child. "I painted them!"

Her name was Susan Waterman, and she was just watching the gallery for the morning while the owner did some errands. They hadn't sold any yet, so it was thrilling that it would happen while she was here. This was her first show. She was actually a botanist at an experimental growing station run by the University of Hawaii.

In the end, overwhelmed by her bubbling gratitude, I bought two paintings, one for Claudie and one for Luisa.

They weren't cheap. Susan also persuaded me to have lunch with her the next day at her studio, where I could look at her latest work and see her garden.

Claudie was strangely quiet when I first gave her the package, wrapped up with the label of the gallery stickered on the outside, but she admired the painting.

"I hope you didn't spend too much, Cassandra."

I was afraid to tell her, and said only, "Got it for a song. It's her first show. Susan Waterman. She's a botanist. She invited me over for lunch tomorrow."

"Leave it to Cassandra," Luisa teased. "If there is a woman to be found, Cassandra will be having lunch with her." She had embraced me violently when I gave her her package, regarding the present, rightly I suppose, as an overture of peace.

Claudie looked as if she were going to say something, but then excused herself, telling us she had a headache.

"I'm sorry," said Luisa. "I think she is, how-do-you-say, *crushed out* on you. It hurts her feelings that you are going to lunch with someone else."

"Don't be ridiculous. Claudie is definitely not *crushed out*. You know she's been upset since the Hana incident. And anyway, it's only lunch."

Susan Waterman lived in a small house outside Lahaina that seemed surrounded by flowering plants, protea, birds-of-paradise, crab's claw ginger. Inside, the walls were covered with sketches and paintings, and on a table was a copy of Georgia O'Keefe's *One Hundred Flowers*.

"I'm a great fan of hers," said Susan, "but it's hard to paint a flower without being influenced by her. Women painted flowers for centuries and it was considered terribly feminine and safe, and then O'Keefe comes along and makes you see everything differently by putting flowers in the foreground and enlarging them so that they push the boundaries of the painting."

On the cover of book was a great white flower, one of the jimson weeds from the Southwest. "Don't you have these too?" I asked.

"Yes," she said. "The name in Hawaiian is Kikania-Haole."

"Doesn't *haole* mean white person?"

Susan laughed. "Yes. Though *haole* used to mean any troublesome foreigner. Maybe that's how it got attached to the jimson weed."

"You'd hardly think of it as a weed," I said.

"That's the marvel of O'Keefe," said Susan. "She makes you see. The critics said her flowers were sexual. O'Keefe said, don't be silly. But they do give you that feeling, a really powerful, self-revelatory eroticism. The petals both explore and close off entry to the inner core."

Underneath her tan, Susan blushed. "I admire O'Keefe so much. She didn't seem to need anybody else. Not like me. I'm always getting mixed up in love affairs, in relationships that are bad for me. Right now, I'm in the midst of deciding to break up and go back to being on my own. To really try to be independent." She fixed me with soft brown eyes that implored me to rescue her from this fate.

"Independence is my middle name," I said. "I've always been independent myself."

She looked disappointed, but tried again, "For me, being independent would mean being financially stable, so I could paint full-time. But unless I strike it rich—or find a sugar girlfriend—I'm afraid that's out of the question."

"Your current girlfriend . . . ?"

". . . misrepresented herself badly," Susan smiled. "But enough about me. Tell me what it's like to be a world traveller and translator."

"Well, I couldn't really support myself without my trust fund," I began, just for the pleasure of seeing the infinitely sweet expression that came into Susan's eyes.

That evening when Claudie had gone out to see her therapist and Luisa and I were back to quarreling bitterly over the translations of tiny three-letter words, the doorbell rang. When I answered it, I found a woman on the doorstep. Before the woman could speak, Luisa called, "Hallo Nell. Claudie isn't here."

"I'm not looking for Claudie."

She wasn't tall, but she was athletic-looking. Her tanned face had a drooping sort of sneer that some might find attractive. Her eyes were blue, a little bloodshot around the iris. She looked about forty, and she looked angry.

"What the hell were you doing with my girlfriend at her place this afternoon?"

"Susan? Your girlfriend?" I stammered. "I bought two of her paintings yesterday. She invited me to lunch, that's all." I was certainly not going to mention those melting brown eyes or the lingering kiss Susan had given me on my departure. I stepped back from the doorway, recalling some karate moves. Luisa was, unfortunately, a total physical coward, so it was no good expecting help from her.

But Nell didn't raise her fists, only her voice. "This is Claudie's way of getting back at me," she said. "I know it. She wanted Susan for herself, and when she couldn't get her, she recruited you."

"Listen, sit down," I said. "Have a glass of water. There's been some terrible misunderstanding. Luisa and I are translating a book, and I thought a flower painting would be a nice present for her. I bought one for Claudie too because she's been so hospitable. Do you think Claudie would have sent me to your gallery on purpose? If you're not on good terms why would she want to give you business?"

For a couple of seconds Nell, considering this, didn't say anything. Then she looked into the room and saw Susan's two framed watercolors propped up against the mantel. Before we could stop her, she'd lifted them up, one after the other, and smashed them, glass and all, on the sharp back of a metal lamp. The delicate pinks and yellows of the hibiscus and plumeria were ripped to shreds.

"You'll get a refund check in the morning," Nell said, and slammed the door as she left.

I was speechless, but Luisa seemed almost admiring. "That kind of passion is common in Uruguay," she said. "You don't see it much in the United States. All those anger management classes."

"She's crazy," I said.

"No," said Luisa. "She's jealous."

III.

The sorceresses of Greek mythology—Hecate, Circe—knew well the narcotic, stimulant, and deadly effects of this plant, and Linnaus gave it the Latin name **Atropa** *after the Greek Goddess of the Underworld Atropos, who cut the thread of life.*

—Dietrich Frohne

I slept on my suspicions overnight and the next morning took Claudie off for a walk along the beach. "Is there any possibility," I said point-blank, "that Nell murdered Donna Hazlitt?"

Claudie's hair blew in a straight line back from her forehead. She didn't say, of course not; she said, "Not the Nell I know. But then, she didn't turn out to be the Nell I knew in the end."

"I don't have a good reason to be suspicious of Nell," I admitted. "I just am. But tell me why you think she might be involved in this in any way."

"That phone call with Mrs. Hazlitt. You remember I said she started in the middle talking about this painting. I'm embarrassed to say I just assumed that she was probably senile and that she somehow thought we'd already met. But afterwards it occurred to me that maybe she really had talked to someone about the painting before."

"And that someone might have been Nell?"

"Our old business cards have both the gallery number and my home number. I kept the house; Nell took the gallery. If Mrs. Hazlitt used the old business card, she might have called Nell the first time, and then tried the home number the second and gotten me."

"But why would Nell kill her to get the painting? Did she want the painting that badly? She must realize she can't sell the painting now; you'd know."

"I'm afraid," said Claudie, staring at the flat blue sea, "that she might have done it for Susan."

So the tangled story came out. How Susan had appeared in their lives, first claiming to be in love with Claudie, and then when Claudie told her she would leave Nell, saying that she was happy to share. How that sharing turned into Nell falling in love with Susan, violently in love, and leaving Claudie.

"Susan doesn't really seem like such a femme fatale," I said conservatively, though I remembered the eager touch of her lips on mine.

"She's not at all," said Claudie. "She's more like a puppy dog that you think you're playing with and all of sudden you realize has wrapped the leash around your legs so you can't move."

She shook her black hair. "And I wasn't even in love with her the way Nell is. Nell is absolutely obsessed with her."

I thought of Susan telling me how her girlfriend, soon to be ex-girlfriend, had misrepresented herself.

"So you think Nell wanted to give her the painting to show her how much she cares? Or to ensure their financial future?

"Oh, I don't know, Cassandra. I lie awake at night, wishing the whole thing had never happened. That poor old woman; she was so excited about her discovery."

"Have you told the police?"

"They don't even believe in the painting; why should they believe that Mrs. Hazlitt was murdered because of it?"

I decided to take Susan up on her invitation to drop by "anytime," but I made sure her car wasn't in the drive first. The little house was locked, but that was no problem for a credit-card carrier like myself. I slipped a card between door and jamb and was inside in a second. It was the middle of the afternoon and I assumed she was at work. I hoped I wouldn't be there long.

Alas, searching for a flower painting in a studio full of flower paintings was harder than it looked. Over and over I thought, Yes! Then, No . . . There were copies of O'Keefe paintings, sketches, and watercolors in great piles. Over and over the same creamy white flowers, close-up angel's trumpets, or jimson weed—or belladonna or Kikania-Haole—whatever you wanted to call it.

After two hours, I had to give up on finding the painting. But I had found something more important perhaps: a scrap of paper in a book called *Poisonous Plants* by Dietrich Frohne, marking an entry on "Datura." According to the book, this is the botanical name of the Jimson Weed in the United States, the Thorn Apple in Britain, the Kikania-Haole in Hawaii. It is a member of the nightshade family, which also includes red peppers, potatoes, and belladonna, to which the jimson weed is closely related. The book also noted that datura seeds had long been used in India for suicide and murder and that criminals had used extracts of the seeds to knock out railway passengers and rob them. The term "Jimson" came from Jamestown, where the weed had led to a mass poisoning in 1676, which effectively wiped out the colony. Taken orally, the datura seeds cause great thirst and a terrible flushing of the skin. They cause the person who ingests them to thrash around and pick randomly at imaginary objects in the air. Further hallucinations follow; then coma and death.

Of course datura is not all bad. For example, atropine comes from the belladonna plant and is useful in dilating the pupil of the eye.

Susan could easily have answered the phone at the gallery and gone to Mrs. Hazlitt's house. She, not Nell, knew the poisonous effects of plants. She, not Nell, would have known how to recognize an O'Keefe painting. She, not Nell, had a financial motive. She wanted to paint full-time.

I left Susan's house with the book under my arm and went straight to the police station.

A year later, months after the trial was finally over and Susan Waterman acquitted for lack of more than circumstantial evidence, I got a letter from Claudie.

By that time I was in Indonesia, staying with my old friend Jacqueline Opal, who had suddenly and enthusiastically taken up a spot in an all-women's gamelan orchestra and was spending all her time bonging away on melodious drums. I had more or less forgotten about my Hawaiian trip (and was avoiding letters from Luisa that quibbled about adverb placement in the proofs of her novel), but Claudie's opening brought it all back:

"They apprehended her at the Honolulu Airport, trying to smuggle out the O'Keefe painting. She confessed everything. How she'd answered the phone at the gallery and talked with Mrs. Hazlitt that first time. The next day when she called Mrs. Hazlitt, she realized the woman had already gotten in touch with me. She raced over to her house that night, frantic that I'd get the painting and she wouldn't. That's when she found out about her eye condition and saw the bottle of atropine in the medicine cabinet. She knew something about atropine because she'd just gotten over an eye infection herself, and her doctor had told her that atropine was poisonous. She made up some story about having heard about echinacea and got Mrs. Hazlitt to offer her some and to take her dose at the same time, from the wrong bottle. She didn't realize it would be such a horrible death, but then, she wasn't there to see it. She had managed to persuade Mrs. Hazlitt to let her take the painting that night. That's why there was no sign of breaking and entering.

"Susan doesn't really blame you, Cassandra, for making her go through the trial and everything. The important thing, she says, is that Nell was caught. Nell says she needed the money because her gallery was failing without me. As usual, she blames everyone else but herself—me for making her business fail, Susan for wanting to break up with her. Nell wanted Susan to be accused of murder so that she would turn back to Nell for support!

"We don't care now. Susan came to live with me last month, and this time I think it's going to work. She's quit her job and I'm supporting her. It's so important for her to paint full-time. As for the O'Keefe painting—oh, it's lovely, an earlier version of *Belladonna—Hana (Two Jimson Weeds)*. One of the flowers has a visible green center. The other has its core hidden, so that your eye is drawn deeper and deeper inside.

"The next time you come to Hawaii you'll have to be sure and see it."

An Expatriate Death

It wasn't the first thing I was supposed to notice about the charming colonial Mexican town of San Andreas, but I did, at the beginning and ever after. When I look back on the whole experience, it's the memory of the high stucco walls and the glass shards embedded in them that comes too readily to mind.

Not every house in San Andreas has that kind of outer walls, of course—the Indian houses don't have them, nor those of most of the Mexicans. The walls were designed mainly to protect the white expatriates, the wealthy ones—those who had moved to San Andreas because it was so picturesque. You had to admit that the broken glass stuck along the tops of the walls was probably more picturesque than barbed wire.

Eleanor Harrington, the woman who was renting me and Lucy her house for a week, had glass-embedded walls, but she was so used to them that she didn't bother to comment as she unlocked the heavy wooden outer door and led us through a patio brimming with bright pots of flowering succulents. Eleanor Harrington was in her early fifties and had pinkish-blond hair, bouffant with thin bangs, milky blue eyes, and a face that was paler than her neck and arms. She wore a cotton embroidered smock, sleeveless and low-necked, over her stretch pants, and her tanned arms were ringed up to the elbow with wide silver bracelets. She'd lived in San Andreas for thirty years, she told us, and had bought this old colonial mansion and had it restored inside and out.

"I really shouldn't be charging you rent at all," she said with the nervous laugh that women often use when they discuss money. "It's really more of a favor to me to have someone here while I go off to see my son in Houston. It's something I do every year, not that I enjoy it much—his wife, you see . . . But I try never to leave my house unattended; it wouldn't be safe."

In spite of us doing her a favor, she was quick enough to take the check that Lucy held out. "Splendid," she said. "What luck that Georgia mentioned you were looking for a place." She glanced at Lucy, and said, "And did she tell me you were a doctor, Ms. Hernandez?"

"Yes," said Lucy.

"Well, I'm sure you'll enjoy yourself *enormously* here," said Eleanor. "It's meant so much to me to be in San Andreas as long as I have. Of course it's changed a great deal, not always for the better, but it's always had a feeling of home to me. There's so much to do culturally. You must look at our little English-language newspaper and see what's going on. There are performances, readings; perhaps you might take a yoga class one day, or even Spanish. You, of course, speak Spanish, Ms. Hernandez . . . where did your parents come from?"

Not smiling back, Lucy said, "San Francisco. San Francisco, California."

Lucy had just spent three months on the Mexican border to Guatemala, working in a refugee camp in a clinic there for mothers and babies. She was on her way back to her job in Oakland, but hearing that I was also planning to pass through Mexico to a conference in Costa Rica, had persuaded me to take a brief holiday with her. An acquaintance of hers, a painter, had raved about San Andreas, and had, in the end, come up with a place for us to rent.

Although I had known Lucy for many years and saw her as frequently as I could, I was struck by the change in her. Her light brown skin was matte and dusty-looking, and her hair, which she usually kept very short, was dry and bushy. She was painfully thin as well.

"I'm just tired," she said, after Eleanor had driven off in her red Toyota for the airport in Mexico City and we were left alone in the living room of the house, with its terra-cotta tiled floor, bright cotton rugs, and shuttered windows. There were weavings on the couches and embroideries on the walls, along with black pottery and the well-known Oaxacan wooden carvings of dogs and other animals, fancifully painted. Some of Eleanor's own sculptures stood among the folk art; they were bronze figures, in the manner of Degas, of Indians, particularly women, often seated, as if at the marketplace.

"We'll put these away while we're here," said Lucy. It was not a question.

And then she went upstairs for a nap although it was only ten in the morning.

I let myself out the locked street door ("Always remember to lock up," were Eleanor's parting words) and went for a walk. Although I'd been in Mexico City a number of times and had explored the southern parts of the country around Oaxaca and the Yucatan, I'd never been in any of the old colonial cities that had been built by the Spanish in the silver-mining days of the seventeenth and eighteenth centuries. There were cobbled streets, pastel- and white-painted buildings with thick walls and inner courtyards dripping with brilliant bougainvillea. There were numerous jewelry, crafts, and clothes shops, clearly catering to tourists and expatriates. You saw them in their shorts and T-shirts, their straw hats and sunglasses, in husband-and-wife couples, alone or in small groups, tan and well-fed, taking up the sidewalks as they passed.

The central square, the zocalo, however, was predominantly Mexican. It had newspaper vendors and people with small carts offering fresh fruit and nuts and candy. On the benches sat men reading papers or in conversation. The arcades on three sides of the square were packed with more vendors, selling the tackier forms of tourist souvenirs—sombreros, T-shirts, and tin jewelry. On the fourth side of the square was a church with a pinkish baroque facade.

I picked up a copy of the Mexico City newspaper, *La Jornada*, as well as the small English-language weekly produced in San Andreas, and chose a cafe down a side street from the zocalo to have a coffee. Unlike some of the other restaurants I'd seen while strolling around, this one didn't have big signs in Gringlish advertising margaritas and superbig enchiladas. The few tables were arranged around a fountain in a small courtyard. There were plenty of plants, a parrot, a simple menu.

After I'd read *La Jornada*, I turned to the San Andreas paper. It had a chatty local tone, much like any small-town newspaper. The comings and goings of prominent San Andreans were noted, including the departure of Eleanor for Houston. There were a couple of art reviews of recent shows, a discussion of some traffic problems in a certain part of town, and mentions of many upcoming events. Eleanor had been right: There was a lot going on here, from yoga classes, to dance workshops, to readings. San Andreas was one of the Mexican towns where people came to learn Spanish. It had at least half a dozen language schools. Over the years a large expatriate community of mostly Americans, but also some Europeans, had built up. Some were older people who'd retired where their social security and pension dollars went a lot further, but many were artists and writers or would-be artists and writers.

I'm an expatriate myself, but I had never lived any place where sizable numbers of expats of the same nationality gathered together. It had always seemed to me that that would defeat the point, which is to leave your country behind.

I was just about to get up and leave when I noticed my name in the paper. For just a second, I thought that it was another comings and goings tidbit, as in Eleanor leaves and Cassandra and Lucy sublet her place. But then I saw that it was embedded in a small piece about a mystery writer, Colin Michaels, who was giving a reading tonight at the local arts center, El Centro Artistico.

"Long-time San Andreas resident Colin Michaels will read from his new mystery, *The Cassandra Caper*. Featuring his intrepid private investigator, Paul Roger, this new book opens with the dead body of a woman, Cassandra Reilly, washed up on a beach in Baja California. Cassandra was a go-go dancer in the 1970s who had fallen on hard times, and it's up to Paul Roger to find the murderer in this exciting new thriller. Colin Michaels has written ten previous novels with Paul Roger."

"Lucy!" I said, when I got back to the house. "Somebody's trying to kill me!"

"What?" She had gotten up from her nap but hadn't progressed much further than a prone position on the sofa. It was as if the muscles and tendons that had been holding her upright had suddenly collapsed, all at once. She was reading an Agatha Christie mystery, in Spanish.

I handed her the local paper, and she read the short notice and began to laugh.

"A go-go dancer, hmm? Of course it's just a coincidence. Reilly's a common name."

"But Cassandra's not! Why do you think I chose it? No, the man must have somehow picked it up from one of the books I've translated. Those Gloria de los Angeles novels are everywhere."

"Well, you can't do anything now," Lucy said. "His novel's been published."

"I'll sue! I'll figure something out. I'll go to his reading and heckle him at least."

It was a useful ruse, anyway, to get Lucy out of the house.

We ate dinner before the reading at a small restaurant I'd noticed near Eleanor's house. We had salads and enchiladas verdes and Tecate beer. Lucy said she could get more authentic food in San Francisco's Mission District, but she ate it. It gave her small comfort to speak Spanish with the waiter.

"I really don't feel I should be here," she said. "It was more wrenching than I imagined to leave the camp. I'd gotten so attached to the people. Cassandra, some of them have been living there for almost ten years, and they have no idea when they'll be able to get back to their villages in Guatemala. The conditions they're living in are tolerable, but that's about all. Just by living in the camps, they're losing their culture."

"You did what you could," I said. Small consolation.

"But I feel so guilty at having left! In three months I did so little. If I didn't have my job in Oakland to get back to, I would have stayed."

Two straight couples came into the restaurant and sat down at the next table. They were middle-aged Americans. Georgia's long letter to Lucy had said, "You'll love how easy it is to meet people in San Andreas—everybody talks to everybody!"

Apparently this was true, for our neighbors had no problems breaking into our conversation, introducing themselves and telling us more than we ever wanted to know about them. The Nelsons, long-time residents of San Andreas, knew Eleanor well. "Oh yes, she's been a real force in San Andreas." They glanced at each other briefly and Mrs. Nelson added brightly, "Without her and Colin, El Centro Artistico never would have gotten off the ground the way it has. People come from everywhere to take classes there."

"We've only been here five years, but we just think it's the best place on earth!" she went on. "Imagine—we've got a maid and a gardener—we'd never be able to afford help in the States, but here we hardly have to pay anything. Bob's got his golf and I'm a volunteer at the library. One of the things we love about San Andreas is that we hardly have to know any Spanish. We're trying to persuade Lois and George to move here. Even with the cost of living going up here, they'll still be able to live so much better than at home."

"I love it," said Lois Palmer. "I've been taking a ceramics class at the arts center, and a cooking class. I love Mexican food, don't you? But George isn't so sure."

"Got a problem with the old ticker," said George. "I know there are a couple of clinics, and one is for people like us, but I'm still not convinced. What if I had a heart attack on the street downtown and ended up at the Mexican clinic?"

Lucy was too disgusted to even bother replying. And even if she had, she'd have been met by shocked surprise. "But we love Mexico and the Mexicans," they would say, puzzled. "They're such warm people, and their culture is so fascinating."

I jumped up with the check. "Well, we're off to a reading tonight," I said.

"That's right," said Mrs. Nelson, "Colin's reading. Well, you're in for a treat!"

El Centro Artistico was a small but beautiful colonial-style structure, built around a courtyard landscaped with trees and plants. We went up a marble staircase to the second floor, where the reading was being held. It surprised me how many people were packed in the little room—a good seventy-five. Almost all of them were white, and many looked retirement age, but there were also a number of younger and middle-aged people. Many of them seemed to know each other and were deep in conversations, of which we caught snatches:

"First chapter is really coming along. Couple of good paragraphs today."

"Did you see what the Wallaces have done to their house? That incredible ceramic work. And they hardly had any trouble with the workmen."

Several people came up to us to chat, intrigued no doubt by the fact that Lucy was Latina ("We want the local people to always feel welcome at our events!"). For the first time in many years, I felt peculiar about introducing myself and resorted to my given name, Catherine Frances.

"Are you an artist?" a woman with thick glasses and a rayon blouse printed with—yes, suitcases—asked me.

"Not even an amateur," I replied.

"Are you here to study Spanish?"

"No," I said reluctantly. No use telling her I made my living as a translator of Spanish literature; that could only lead to a discussion of the books I'd worked on and the revelation of my name. And I couldn't bear the news to spread so soon around the room, that I had become a fictional character.

"Cassandra—or what had been Cassandra—was a worn-out bundle of varicose veins, needle tracks, and bunions. Her mottled face hung slackly and even under the water you could see that she had a bad dye job."

Colin Michaels had been reading for about fifteen minutes when I decided to murder him. A short, red-faced man in his sixties, with a silky pompadour of white hair, he wore a short-sleeved Mexican shirt open in a V that showed his tan chest and white chest hair.

His character, Paul Roger, was different. Lanky, tough, laconic. You couldn't call Colin Michaels laconic by any stretch of the imagination. In fact, I began to think he was never going to shut up.

Finally he finished reading and it was time for questions. In order he got: "Do you use a computer?" "How old were you when you started writing?" "How do you get an agent?" and "Have any of your books been made into films?" and then came one of those long-winded questions that isn't really a question but more a statement— if only you could figure out about what—on the part of the questioner.

Eventually it was my turn.

"I'm curious about where you came up with the name Cassandra Reilly for your victim."

"It's a great name, isn't it?" he said happily. "I have an Irish background myself so Reilly was obvious, but I think the choice of *Cassandra* was really quite inspired. Cassandra was the daughter of the King of Troy, who had the gift of prophecy, but not of being believed."

"I *know* who the mythical Cassandra was, thank you," I interrupted. "But did you realize that Cassandra Reilly is the real name of someone—someone I know quite well actually—yes, a very esteemed translator, the translator of Gloria de los Angeles's magic realism novels. I'm sure the *real* Cassandra Reilly will be horribly upset when she hears that her name has been *stolen* and appended to the name of some dead go-go dancer!"

I sat down with a thump.

"Well, if I'm any judge of character," said Colin Michaels with a genial wink, "your friend will be flattered, not offended, to have her name appear in print."

A wave of mild laughter, meant to support Colin and dismiss me, flowed through the room, and he went on to the next question.

"I'm writing a mystery," a man said. "And I know I need to know about guns. I've read up on them, but I feel like I need to actually see one, to hold one, to fire one . . ."

"To murder someone . . ." a voice added and everyone laughed.

"Do you have a gun?" the voice persevered. "Have you used one?"

Colin gave his genial smile. "Haven't you heard?" he said, "We mystery writers are the least violent people around. We keep it all in our heads!"

Sometime after midnight that night there was a loud banging on the outside gate. Lucy was up and ready for bad news before I'd gotten my bathrobe on. When I finally managed to get downstairs, I saw her leading two uniformed policemen into the house.

"They found Eleanor off the highway to Mexico City," said Lucy in a flat tone. "In a motel room."

"What do you mean, they found her?" I stumbled and sat down on a woven footstool. "You mean, she wasn't really going to Houston at all? She was having a tryst?"

"When they found her she was dead," said Lucy, still trying to take it in. "Someone shot her through the heart."

The police grilled us for an hour or two, not because they believed we were particularly guilty of anything, but because we might be able to give them information about Eleanor that would explain her death.

According to the police, the motel was a cheesy but not completely down-and-out place on the outskirts of Mexico City, near the airport, about four hours away from San Andreas. Had Eleanor just gone there to rest before her flight? It seemed likely, because she'd asked the reception clerk to give her a wake-up call at 10 p.m. When she didn't answer after several attempts, he knocked on the door, and finally, worried, let himself in. She'd been dead for several hours then. Had it been a random murder? A robbery as well? The police were inclined to think so. Her bags had been rifled through; so had the glove compartment of her car. It looked as if some jewelry might be missing. The Mexico City police were questioning all the motel's employees.

We couldn't help the police other than to let them look around Eleanor's house and take her address book. One of them, Officer Delgado, called her son's house in Houston. He began by speaking English but switched to Spanish in a minute.

When he put down the phone, he said that her relatives would be flying in tomorrow.

"He spoke Spanish to you," I commented.

"No, her son was away on business," said Delgado. "That was his wife."

At seven the next morning, Eleanor's housekeeper Rosario let herself in. She hadn't heard the news yet, and had to sit down at first when we told her. "What a terrible death," she said, making the sign of the cross. Rosario was about Eleanor's age, perhaps a little younger. She had smooth black hair in a bun, and a sturdy, slow-moving body. We thought she would want to go home, but instead, after a glass of water, she rose and began the work of dusting and straightening, all the while murmuring, "How terrible."

We watched for a moment, unsure whether she was mourning Eleanor the person or just reacting to the horror of the situation. "I'm not sure you need to do anything now," Lucy told her gently.

"But people will be coming," Rosario said. "Her son will finally come back now, and Isabella."

"Isabella?" I asked. "Is that his wife?"

"Yes," said Rosario, "She comes from San Andreas."

Eleanor's death sent a chill of fear through the expatriate community. In whispered conversations in the expensive restaurants and shops, they told each other that they weren't surprised. The flip side of their belief that the Mexicans were warm and happy people was their conviction that the whole country seethed with thieves and murderers. That afternoon Colin Michaels called a community meeting at El Centro Artistico, and the room was packed.

"We've got to pressure the police to solve this murder quickly," he said. "The Mayor of San Andreas is at the coast at the moment, but his assistant agrees—the death of one American is a horrible blow to the image of Mexican tourism."

Colin's face was flushed a strawberry color, and his voice was shrill. "A member of our peaceful little community has been murdered," he said. "We could be next!"

I bumped into him on purpose after the meeting. "Oh, the friend of Cassandra Reilly's," he said. "I'm sorry, I didn't catch your name. You and your friend have been staying at Eleanor's. How very upsetting for you."

"You knew her well, it sounds like," I said.

"Oh everyone knew Eleanor," he said. "She was a fixture. An absolute fixture. We discovered San Andreas years ago, both of us. We were the early ones. We had a chance to really mold it to become the place it is now. Without Eleanor, this arts center wouldn't exist. I can't believe, I just can't believe she's gone."

"Then you know about her son and his wife," I said. "What was that story again?"

"I always liked the girl myself," said Colin. "It was her mother, her whole family, that was the problem. Greedy, always taking advantage of whatever kindness Eleanor showed them. The girl herself . . ."

"Isabella?"

"Yes. She was so young. It was her mother who had ambitions, who made sure to leave the two young people together so that the inevitable happened."

"Isabella's mother is local then?"

"Why yes. You must have met her. Rosario, the woman who cleans—cleaned—for Eleanor."

I remembered Rosario's stunned face but deep-down lack of feeling about Eleanor's death, how her dark eyes had looked past us to something on a table or a shelf, something terribly familiar, that was now missing. "Where are the figures?" she had asked. "Señora Harrington's sculptures?"

"I put them away yesterday," Lucy had admitted. "I didn't . . . like to look at them."

"Ah," Rosario had said. "*Bueno.*"

When I got back to the house I found Lucy talking with the gardener. "This is Isabella's brother, Juan," she said. "He has a degree in English literature but hasn't been able to find work."

Juan wore a Grateful Dead T-shirt and an earring in one ear. "My sister is always trying to get me to come to the States to live. I don't mind visiting, but I wouldn't want to live there. I'd rather live in my own country. Not that San Andreas always feels like Mexico."

"Did the whole family work for Eleanor?" I asked Lucy when Juan had left for the day. "And if Rosario and Juan were her relatives as well as her employees, why would Eleanor feel she needed people to housesit for her?"

"I don't know whether it was a question of trust, or of trying to make a few extra dollars. Do you remember how quick she snatched up our check yesterday?"

"But she has tons of money! Doesn't she? She must just employ them as a favor to her son."

Her son. Something that had been nagging at me all day rose to the surface. "And where was he in the middle of the night anyway? Away on business. Does anyone know where?"

Isabella and her two young daughters arrived that night after dinner and came straight to the house. Lucy and I were ready to leave, but she insisted we stay.

"No, you must stay, please," she said. "Allen would want it."

"But at a time like this—we'd only be in the way."

"At least until tomorrow," she said urgently.

I wondered if she were afraid to stay in the house by herself.

Isabella was an attractive woman of about thirty, dressed for travel in a simple dress and sandals. Her black hair was fashionably cut and she had a warm but slightly imposing air. I couldn't imagine her putting up with any shit from Eleanor.

After she got her two girls off to bed, she came back downstairs, now wearing jeans, her eyes taking in the room as she descended.

"It hasn't changed," she said. "In ten years, it hasn't really changed. Still the beautiful home I admired in my silly way when I used to come here with my mother to help her clean it. Everything so tasteful, so beautiful. So artistic, I thought. The home of an artist." She laughed shortly. "But what happened to her sculptures, all those Indian women in serapes with their baskets full of tortillas?"

"I put them away," said Lucy.

Isabella sat down, but her tiredness didn't cause her to slump. "I'm embarrassed to tell you that I really liked them, that summer I was twenty. I didn't have much consciousness about anything. Allen was just about as innocent as I was. 'Oh, my mother will adore you,' he kept telling me.

"My own mother told me different, but I didn't pay any attention to her. She was right, of course, not Allen. When Eleanor came back from her vacation and found out what had been going on for two months, she threw me out. She couldn't believe that Allen followed. She never believed it. Even when she came for her annual visit to Houston, she tried not to see me or the kids if she could avoid it."

"Where is Allen by the way?" I put in, as casually as I could.

Isabella's eyes shifted slightly, but her tone seemed straightforward. "He was a little hard to track down. As a matter of fact, he's right here in Mexico. In Cancun. He's driving up to San Andreas tonight." She took a long breath, which made me realize she'd been holding it. "The company he works for, a hotel chain, is always sending him on the road."

"You realize, he's the one who did it," I told Lucy that night when we were alone. "He must have hated his mother for what she did to his wife."

"It takes a lot more than hatred to kill someone," said Lucy, from the twin bed next to me. "Sure he 'disappointed' her by marrying a Mexican, but why would he kill his mother over it ten years later? If he really did kill her, it was for some other reason. Money, for instance. How well-off was Eleanor really, and what about Allen himself? Is he in debt? Does he have a drug habit? Would inheriting Eleanor's money help him?" Lucy held up the Agatha Christie she was reading. "I used to read lots of these in medical school. They probably gave me a distorted view of crime—that it was all about entailed estates and hidden relatives—but at bottom they said something true—people are more likely to kill for money than for passion."

Allen Harrington had still not arrived by the time I woke up in the morning and headed out for my morning coffee. Lucy got up at the same time and went off to the local clinic. "I'll just have them check me out," she said. "And then, maybe, I'll see if they need me to volunteer at all while we're here."

"You just can't keep away from work," I teased her, but I was still worried. What if there was something really wrong with her?

As luck would have it, I discovered Colin Michaels in the cafe I'd gone to yesterday. He was drinking a large Bloody Mary and eating eggs and bacon. No wonder every capillary on his face was broken.

"Hello, friend of Cassandra Reilly," he greeted me. "We've got to stop meeting like this."

"Tell me about Eleanor's son," I said, sitting down next to him and ordering *café con leche*. "You said you'd known her since the early days here. You must have known her son when he was growing up."

"Oh, he didn't grow up here," said Colin, a little too quickly. "I mean, he came in the summers. But otherwise, he went to a boarding school in the States. Eleanor didn't want him to go to school in San Andreas. She wanted him to have a proper education."

"If Eleanor was around fifty and her son is around thirty," I said, thinking aloud, "She must have been fairly young when she had him."

"I suppose so," said Colin, bending over his food.

"What about Mr. Harrington?" I said suddenly. "Nobody says anything about a Mr. Harrington. I always assumed that Eleanor had gotten her money from her husband, that she was a wealthy widow."

"Believe the money came from her family," said Colin. "Parents set her up here, wanted her out of Houston, I suppose. But myself, I've always believed that the past is past. We all have our reasons to have settled in San Andreas. Now, myself . . ."

"Oh, I see," I said slowly. "Yes, of course. There was no Mr. Harrington. Eleanor's son Allen was born out of wedlock."

"What's past is past," said Colin and ordered another drink. It was only nine in the morning.

You could be a drunk anywhere, but it must be more pleasant, and cheaper, in San Andreas.

Allen Harrington drove up at noon. Did I have a reason for assuming he'd be white? Only my own ethnocentrism. He was a compact, dark-skinned man, darker than his wife, with startling green eyes.

"What a nightmare," he said, as he paced around the room. "What a way for my mother to die. Have they found out anything more about the man who killed her? I'm going down to the police station in a few minutes. I'll make them take this seriously."

Don't overdo it, Allen, I thought.

Isabella tried to soothe him. "I'm sure the police are doing all they can."

"But what kind of a country is this, that people can't check into a motel room without being robbed and murdered?"

"The police seem to think she knew her attacker," I said, and Lucy stared at me to hear such a bold-faced lie.

"They do?" Allen shouted at his wife. "You didn't tell me this. Who killed my mother? Juan? Your worthless cousin Pedro?"

For answer, Isabella turned on her heel and marched out of the house.

"That was a harsh thing to say," said Lucy.

Allen stared at us a moment and then, unable to defend himself, he burst into agitated tears.

When he calmed down, he said, "I loved my mother. I know she wasn't a particularly good person. In some ways, I admit, she wrecked my life. But she was still my mother."

"Who was your father, Allen?" I asked.

"I don't know. My mother may not have known herself. She came down to Mexico when she was nineteen or twenty for a few weeks of partying, and ended up getting pregnant. By the time she realized it, she was too far along for an abortion. The Harringtons are a prominent family in Houston. The agreement was that if she stayed in Mexico, they'd set up a trust fund for her, and she agreed. It was a crazy mix of shame and pride that kept her here. She loved Mexico and she hated it. The only way she could stay here was to stay separate and to bond with the other white expatriates. She never felt quite accepted here though—that's why she sent me away to school."

Allen looked at his arm, which was the color of walnut. "She couldn't ever really see me, see who I was. When I wanted to marry Isabella, she said, 'You can't marry a Mexican.'

"'Mother,' I said. 'I *am* a Mexican.'

"'No you're not,' she said. 'You're white. You don't even speak Spanish. You have dual citizenship. You belong in America.'

"I didn't speak much Spanish then. Meeting Isabella changed me. I learned Spanish and found a job that would let me travel in Mexico."

"Isabella said you were in Cancun."

He looked at me oddly, and almost aggressively, with those brilliant green eyes. "You need proof? You think *I* was somehow involved in this?"

"Don't be ridiculous," broke in Lucy calmly. "Cassandra was just asking a question."

"I'm sorry," he said, calming down. "I apologize. And now, if you'll excuse me," he said. "I also need to apologize to my wife."

Dr. Rodriguez, Antonia Rodriguez, the head doctor at the local clinic, had said Lucy seemed to be suffering from exhaustion and a slight case of anemia, nothing more. But she had sent a blood sample to Mexico City anyway. Meanwhile she didn't exactly say no to Lucy helping her out a couple of hours every morning. The clinic was seriously underfunded, unlike the private clinic that the expatriates all went to.

"It makes me feel better to do something," Lucy said. "Otherwise I'd go crazy here."

But even working two hours was tiring to her, and when she came back to the small hotel where we'd moved after Allen arrived, she usually lay on the bed reading Agatha Christie.

I kept waiting for the police to announce that Allen Harrington had killed his mother. Who else would have known she was stopping at that motel? Who else would have persuaded Eleanor to open her door to him?

But days passed and no murder suspect was named.

The next issue of the local English paper came out with an angry editorial by Colin Michaels and with letters to the editor that bemoaned the days when San Andreas had been a safe little town. "I left Los Angeles because of the crime . . . and what do I find here?"

There was a small notice near the back of the paper that made me pause. It said that the bulk of Mrs. Harrington's estate would go toward expanding the arts center. An auditorium for readings would be added, and a new library specializing in English books. Colin Michaels, president of the board of El Centro Artistico, expressed his pleasure and said that, in honor of Eleanor's bequest, the new center would be named after Mrs. Harrington.

I decided to visit the little newspaper office and asked for the managing editor.

"I don't know what their relationship was," she admitted. "I've only been here a few years, and Colin and Eleanor went back thirty years. You might talk to one of the past editors. Dora James started the paper in the early seventies. She remembers everything."

"Oh, they had quite the feud going once," Dora James said. "Eleanor had the money, but Colin had the name. He was one of the biggest names to settle in San Andreas. Not that he was so incredibly successful anyplace but here. But that's one reason people settle here, you know. In the States, Colin was just another mystery writer; here he was famous. They both wanted to control the arts center. This year Colin was president, but last year she was. It was essentially harmless, their bickering and wrangling. Though I must admit, I'd heard that the victim in Colin's latest novel, *The Cassandra Caper*, was an unflattering portrait of Eleanor. He must feel terrible now. Especially since she left the arts center all that money."

Well, at least I knew now that Eleanor really had been rich. But where did her giving most of her money to the arts center leave Allen?

Dora James shook her head. "Have you ever read any of Colin's mysteries? They really don't improve. I always end up feeling as if I've missed something crucial in understanding the plot. But it's usually because Colin has forgotten it himself. What he needs, you know," she smiled, "is a good editor."

I found Allen with Isabella in the house, where they were packing up Eleanor's things. "Yes, I know about the bequest," he said. "The house is mine though. We're giving it to Rosario."

107

I asked him if his mother ever talked much about Colin Michaels.

"Oh, old Colin," said Allen. "They were lovers all during my childhood. They had a terrible fight sometime during the seventies. They'd helped create the arts center together, you see. But they couldn't agree how to run it. The last I heard, Mother was going to pull all her money out of it. She told me she'd been talking to a lawyer in Mexico City. I didn't believe that she really would. It was just something she used against Colin. Her feud with him had been going on for years. But the arts center really meant something to her. And judging from her will, she really did want almost everything to go into expanding it."

I didn't know how to ask for the name of the lawyer, but he gave it to me anyway as he went on, "One of the maids at the motel where my mother was killed says she saw a man with a black mustache and dark hat slipping down the corridor sometime late in the afternoon that day. I thought maybe it could have been my mother's lawyer, Jorge Salinas, because he has a big black mustache, but his secretary confirmed he'd been in his office all day. It was probably just something the maid made up to make herself sound more interesting."

When I called Jorge Salinas, he admitted that Mrs. Harrington was his client, and that she had talked to him recently, but he couldn't tell me about what. They'd had no appointment the day she was murdered, he told me. His records could confirm it.

I pressed further. "I know you can't tell me what you and Mrs. Harrington discussed. That's confidential of course. But let me pose it this way, so that you can just answer yes or no. If there was someone who had an interest in keeping El Centro Artistico alive and that person found out that Eleanor Harrington planned to pull her money out of it . . ."

"This does not sound like a simple yes or no question, but go on."

"Wouldn't it have been in that person's interest, given the will, if Mrs. Harrington died before she could financially withdraw or change her will?"

He was silent.

"Let me put it this way. Given the circumstances, and given what you may know about the people in her life, did Mrs. Harrington's death come as a complete surprise?"

"No," he said finally. "No, it did not."

It was time to go to the police. Delgado was skeptical. "Señor Michaels has an alibi for the time Mrs. Harrington was murdered. He was here in San Andreas, reading to a large crowd, in a program that had been arranged for weeks."

"Mrs. Harrington left San Andreas at ten in the morning. At a little before two she checked into the motel. You think she died around six. But what if she died earlier, at three? That would have given him four hours to get back to San Andreas."

"It's a possibility," Delgado allowed. "But there are no witnesses."

"Get a search warrant," I said. "It can't do any harm. If Colin is the mystery writer Dora James says he is, he will have made a mistake in his plotting and forgotten some crucial little element. He's no Agatha Christie."

At first I thought I'd made a bad mistake. The police searched Colin's house and car for four hours and found nothing incriminating. No weapon. None of Eleanor's jewelry. No tell-tale copy of a will that she was carrying to her lawyer. It was only by chance that one of the cops happened to open the freezer. There, back in the corner, was a false black mustache, that for reasons of vanity or foolishness, Colin had not been able to bring himself to throw away.

The maid identified him and even though he never confessed, insisting that the mustache was a joke left over from Halloween, Colin soon found himself in the courtroom and then in prison, a place he'd always described from the outside. The Harrington Arts Center expanded without him, though apparently he continues to write murder mysteries from prison while appealing his life sentence.

I heard all this from Lucy, who made a fast friend of Dr. Antonia Rodriguez, the doctor at the San Andreas clinic. Lucy visits her regularly, on her way to and from the refugee camp on the Guatemala border, where she now spends three months every year.

Wie Bitte?

Quickborn.
Schlump.
Poppenbüttel.

I stared at a map of Hamburg's subway system. My destination was one stop beyond Schlump, Marianne had said. Marianne Schnackenbusch was a translator acquaintance I'd run into at the Frankfurt Book Fair a week before. When she heard that we were both translating Gloria de los Angeles's latest collection of short stories—she into German, I into English—she'd generously told me that I must come to stay with her in Hamburg after the fair. She and her partner Elke had loads of room, and I could stay as long as I liked.

It sounded perfect. I had a brief engagement in Paris first, but after that I was at loose ends. My translation was due at the end of November, and I didn't have the money to go anywhere splendid to finish it. Certainly I could have stayed in my small attic room in Nicola's house in London, but in truth I'd been rather avoiding Nicola since the arrival of the Croatian lesbian commune last summer. How was I to know that my blithe offer many years ago to reciprocate their hospitality in Zagreb meant that all six of them would turn up on Nicola's doorstep in July?

Marianne and Elke's flat was in an old area of the city called the Schanzenviertel. Leafy streets, tall graceful apartment buildings, graffiti, bikes everywhere, Turkish and

Greek shops just opening up. I'd taken a night train from Paris and it was still early.

Marianne embraced me heartily at the door. "Please sit down, sit down and eat. You must be starving, all night on the train. You should have told us when you were coming. We could have picked you up."

She was a big woman, with a mane of hennaed red-purple hair around a broad, eager face. She was barefoot and wearing a red silk robe. I knew from our brief talks at bookfairs that she was the daughter of a German Communist who had fled to Chile before the war, and a Chilean mother. She had told me that in addition to translating she also was a lecturer at the university in Latin American literature. I could see from the hallway that translation and teaching must pay better in Germany than in Britain: the flat looked enormous and was full of Oriental carpets and big leather sofas and chairs. There were bookshelves up to the tall ceilings.

"She's a bit overwhelming," my friend Lucinda in Paris had told me. "A combination of Latin American vivacity and Prussian forcefulness. But she's generous to a fault; she'll take care of you well." Lucinda was as poor as I was and knew the value of visits to people with washer-dryers and fax machines. Lucinda sublet a studio about the size of an elevator carriage, and practiced one of the few literary occupations to pay less than translation: poetry.

Elke was already sitting at the kitchen table, which was spread with a huge number of plates of meats and cheeses and jars of spreads and preserves. She was much frailer-looking than Marianne—and older too—with narrow shoulders, short gray-blonde hair and round small glasses. If you didn't see her wrinkles, she would remind you of a boyish Bolshevik in a Hollywood film about the Russian Revolution.

"Just coffee for now," I said.

"No, no," said Marianne, pushing all manner of things toward me, and settling herself. "No, you must eat. This is so exciting for me, having Gloria's English translator here.

There's so much I want to talk over with you. I'm enjoying the stories so much; they just go like the breeze."

I looked across the table in astonishment. We hadn't had time in Frankfurt to discuss the literary value of Gloria's work. I had only assumed she felt the same ambivalence I did. "Well, I always find Gloria to be fairly easy to translate," I said cautiously. "There is a certain . . . similarity in all her work."

"Yes," said Marianne, delicately spreading layers of soft cheese on half a roll and then devouring it in a gulp. "That's what I enjoy so much, how you can always count on her to write so lusciously. Other writers seem dry next to her, while she is sensual, opulent, rich, and vivid. I just sink into her books like a big feather bed, like a warm bath with perfume."

"They do tend to have something of a bathetic effect," I murmured.

"Yes, exactly," said Marianne, but Elke said, "Cassandra means they're sentimental drivel, my friend. And I'm afraid I agree."

"No, she doesn't mean that," Marianne said good-humoredly. "After all, Cassandra has translated all Gloria's books into English."

Elke fortunately changed the subject. "I must be off soon to work. I wish I could stay and help Marianne show you around the city. But we have some problems at work that are rather worrisome."

"Not just the usual problems between the bosses and workers," said Marianne indignantly. "Threats. Terrible threats."

"But don't you work in a bird-watching society?" I asked, uncertain if Marianne had given me the right information or if I'd understood it properly.

"Yes, yes," said Elke. "Well, that's what it was when it was originally founded. Sort of like your Audubon Society in America, I think. But you can't watch birds nowadays without seeing how they are threatened by the loss of their habitats and so forth, and that has made some of the members very activist. We are trying to purchase land and writing letters to the politicians, as well as planning a big demonstration in two weeks. And of course some members are nervous about all this activism, which to them is like confrontation with the state."

"But who is threatening whom?"

"Our whole organization got a threat in the mail, several threats. The first two weeks ago, and another last week, and yesterday one more. It's about the cause we are working on now, trying to save a stretch of the Elbe River. It used to be that this section, not so far from Hamburg, marked the boundary between East and West Germany, and so it was never developed. If you go there, you see old farms and very little else. But now, with reunification, they want to build on either side, and worse—from our point of view, from the birds' point of view, that is—they want to dredge the river to make it deeper, and make concrete sides and so forth, for shipping."

Elke got up. "We don't want this to happen, of course. There is very little left in Europe of undeveloped land, especially wetlands. So we're fighting." She wrapped a scarf several times around her neck and put on her jacket. "And someone doesn't like it."

As soon Elke left, Marianne began talking about Gloria's writing again. "Just now I'm translating the story of the servant girl and the colonel," she said.

"Oh yes, that one."

"What a sly sense of humor Gloria has, don't you think?"

"Well . . ."

"But that's what I admire so much about Gloria. She is capable of slyness and subtlety, and also of great exuberance and broad strokes. She has such a large talent."

"Broad strokes, yes," I said weakly.

Marianne polished off the rest of the rolls and several more cups of coffee, chattering all the while about Gloria. She then showed me to my room, which was large and light. It overlooked an interior garden where the lindens and ashes were turning gold and yellow. "Here is the desk where you will work," she said. It was old-fashioned, of walnut, a desk I had always dreamed of, with green blotting paper and a desk lamp with a warm brown paper shade. A tall bookshelf along one wall was filled with novels in French and Spanish. There was a red Turkish rug on the floor and a daybed covered with pillows.

"I hope this is all right," Marianne said anxiously.

"It's wonderful!"

"And the best thing is, at night, after you are finished translating your Gloria and I am finished translating my Gloria, we will have long evenings to discuss her."

But today there was to be no work. Today Marianne had decided to show me the city of Hamburg. She drove me by the university and through parks with lakes and parks with statues. She bought me an expensive lunch at a restaurant just off the Rathaus Square and told me everything she knew about Hamburg's history, which was quite a lot.

The stories she told me were reflected in the layers of the city: the few timbered buildings with a medieval touch, the tall, narrow buildings along Dutch-looking canals, squeezed in among modern offices in the international style. The city had a grandeur that was more in its substantialness than in any great elegance. It looked like a city where business was done and had always been done. It looked solid, commercial, successful. And yet this air of solidity and permanence was illusory too. For since the Middle Ages, the city had been destroyed over and over by fire, and during the last war the Allied bombings had flattened huge swathes of the city.

The harbor, the heart of Hamburg, where Marianne was taking me now, had been practically destroyed in those bombings. You would not guess it now. Huge container ships from around the world snaked slowly by, escorted by pilot boats. Around them, smaller working and pleasure boats churned up the river water that, on this bright fall day and from this distance, looked blue-green and sparkling. We strolled along the promenade and came to the inner harbor, where Marianne said she had a surprise for me.

Barbara Wilson

"It's funny," I said, looking around me at the huge brick warehouses and the multitude of wooden docks. "I've never been here, and yet it seems familiar."

"A dream?"

"No," I said, suddenly remembering, "It was . . . it was a language course, on British television, many years ago, when I was first in London. It wasn't an ordinary language course; it had a continuing plot, and it took place in Hamburg, around the red-light district and the harbor."

"So you do know German!"

"*Wie Bitte?*" That was the name of the program, which translated as simply, "Please?" or "How's That Again?"

I admitted, "Actually, I didn't progress very far with the lessons. I would usually get too caught up in the plot to remember that I was supposed to be listening for grammatical constructs. So then, after fifteen minutes of action, there would be questions—'What was Peter doing in the red-light district that evening?' 'What did Astrid say when the killer pulled out his gun and shoved her in the back of the boat?'—I could never answer them."

"But your German will come back if we practice it," said Marianne, as she marched me down a flight of metal stairs to a wooden dock alongside one of the harbor walls. "Here it is." She stopped in front of a boat called *The Juliette*. "It's Elke's boat. Actually, Elke owns it with some others, all of whom work for the bird-watching society. It's become the official ship of their movement. They take it out on the Elbe with banners and invite journalists and TV stations."

We stepped down onto the boat and Marianne unlocked the cabin. It was a beautiful old cruiser, roomy enough for ten or twelve people, with a small sleeping area and a minuscule toilet behind the pilot's cabin.

"I wish the others who used the boat would pick up after themselves a bit better," said Marianne, reaching for a bucket and rope that had been left in the middle of the captain's room. "Elke always leaves it spotless."

"Oh no," she said, when she saw the contents of the bucket. It was a seagull with its neck twisted by a metal coil.

116

A piece of paper was attached to the metal, but its message was so wet with blood it was hardly decipherable.

Marianne turned the color of her hair. "This is really the limit. I don't think they should be trying to keep this quiet anymore. They should call the media right away."

"What about the police?"

"Yes, them too. Not that I trust them to be helpful."

I watched as Marianne put the bucket on the dock. I expected that we would follow it and that she would start looking for the nearest phone booth. But instead she turned the key in the engine, which started up with a promising rumble.

"If they think they're going to destroy my pleasure in showing my friend the harbor and the river, they're mistaken. We'll deal with this when we return."

It was an amazing thing to be out on the river among all the other boats. The container ships towered above us like apartment buildings, and even the tugboats seemed five times as large. The water, close now, was pale green, slightly dirty, with a smell that was more river than salt. We cruised past the promenade above and the port of Hamburg buildings, very grand and rounded, and then past the city, in the direction of the faraway sea, and Marianne pointed out restaurants and villas, beaches where there had once been swimming, and the large, brightly painted asylum ships that held foreigners who had come to Germany hoping for refuge or economic opportunity.

Outward bound, Marianne was in determinedly high spirits, telling stories of the river and trips they'd made, relating political problems with gusto and anger, and turning the subject again and again back to Gloria de los Angeles and her large talent.

"I tell you," she said over the roar of the engine, "I have very little patience for some of these fiction writers who are deliberately obscure. I grew up in a very political family, my father was friends with Neruda, and I have always believed that writing should serve the people and be very accessible. There's another Latin American woman writer, for example, whom some people rave about, but who I have absolutely no time for. They have asked me to translate her books, and I tell them, Why bother? She is self-indulgent and obtuse for no reason. I hope she never gets translated into German. We have enough of those kinds of writers already."

"You don't mean Luisa Montiflores?"

"Exactly! You know her?"

"She . . ." Actually, I had received a letter from Luisa only a few days ago. She'd found out from Nicola that I was in Germany and was demanding my help in finding a German translator. "Since you're there, you must have contacts," she wrote.

"Hey! Look out! Get out of our way! Whew. Now would you like a lesson in steering?"

That took all our energy for a while, and in truth, I found it exhilarating, if a bit terrifying, piloting *The Juliette* along the huge waterway. But as we came back into the inner harbor, I could see that Marianne was brooding more and more about the bird with the broken neck.

"Whoever these people are, they're monsters," she burst out finally.

"Who is it who wants to develop that stretch of the Elbe?"

"That's just it. Many corporations, shippers, industrialists stand to gain from it. They're so powerful anyway, why would they resort to such cheap, ugly tricks?"

"They must be more afraid of Elke and her group than you realize."

"Well, I'm calling Elke and getting her to stage a press conference with that poor bird. As soon as we get back."

But when we returned to *The Juliette's* berth, the bucket had vanished.

That evening there was a meeting in Marianne and Elke's flat, attended by eight of the core birdwatchers. Several were mild looking older people, and only one was under thirty—a quiet, bald-headed woman with astonishing tattoos. Two men came together, one very tall and one very round, and a middle-aged couple brought a new baby. They were the only two whose names I caught, Karin and Helmut. The baby was named Sappho, which seemed promising, though she did have an uncommonly pointed head. Marianne decided to take part in the meeting, but I retired to my room, so as not to be in the way, and was soon working on my translation under the light of the lamp at the beautiful desk.

Maybe I *was* too much of an elitist. Gloria's books had reached millions of people and given them a great deal of enjoyment. Who was I to judge? Maybe my long years of association with Luisa Montiflores, who hated Gloria de los Angeles and everything she stood for with a terrible passion, had made it impossible for me to look at Gloria objectively. I reread the paragraph I was translating:

> "He took her passionately; she responded as if in a dream. They coupled frenetically, hour after hour, without eating, without drinking any more than each other's torrid sweat. Days passed, weeks. One day he got up, as if an alarm clock had rung. He looked at his beard in the mirror, at his wasted feverish limbs. And he left.

It was sort of like a warm bath, scented with patchouli oil. But it was not great literature. I must hold my ground. Actually, I must state my true opinion before I could hold it. But I trembled.

About an hour into the meeting, baby Sappho began crying, a noise that started far off down the hall in the living room and came closer, until it remained outside my closed door. In between the shrieks were the voices of her two parents, who started out trying to calm her down but seemed to move into another topic: problems with the way the birdwatchers' meeting was going. Helmut, who had seemed sweet and eager to please when I met him, the very picture of a proud, forty-five-year-old father, sounded very aggrieved indeed, though it was hard, because of my limited German, to understand why. Karin seemed defensive. The only words I caught were "capitalists," and "politizei."

Too bad I hadn't paid more attention long ago to that *Wie Bitte?* series. Why not? I willed myself back many years, to Bayswater, to the small shabby parlor of the house where I'd been staying with a girlfriend and her mother (right from the beginning, no place of my own!). I'd met the girl in Madrid and had followed her to London. She was working as a translator, which I thought so fascinating that I decided to try it myself. She was actually quite a boring girl. Her idea of a good time was to sit at home watching language programs. My idea of a good time was to figure out how to get her mind off television. Her mother had eventually asked me to leave—when the series wasn't even over yet!

Sappho finally grew calm, and the pair went back to the meeting. Eventually everyone left, and it sounded like even Elke and Marianne had gone to bed. To my surprise, I ran into Elke on my way to the bathroom, and she was dressed to go out. It was almost midnight. She looked more like a Russian revolutionary than ever, in her black leather jacket, Palestinian scarf, and leather cap.

"I'm going to sleep on the boat tonight with one of the others," she explained. "We want to make sure that nothing happens to *The Juliette.* We're planning a demonstration this weekend on the Elbe with several boats, and *The Juliette* is to lead them."

"What is the nature of the threatening letters?" I asked. "Has the group been able to come up with any ideas about who wrote them?"

"*Who* actually wrote them and who they want us to think has written them might be two very different things."

"What do you mean?"

"They seem to me to be written by an educated person trying to sound simple-minded. They're in computer type, but with a few words misspelled. Come," she said, and led me back into the comfortable living room where Marianne was listening to the stereo with earphones on and a pile of papers beside her. She looked like a large red bear in her dressing gown. "I'm reading student translations," she shouted happily.

Elke took up a folder from the coffee table and pulled out a computer-printed letter. "Here's the first one: BIRD-LOVERS BEWAR. YOU CAN NEVER WIN AGAINST US. GIVE UP BEFORE YOU ARE SORRY."

She held up another. "And later on they write, IF YOU GO ON WITH THE PLANED DEMONSTRASION, YOU WILL REGRET IT."

"They do seem sort of fake, don't they?" I agreed. "But how did he or she know about the demonstration?"

"A good question, since we had at that point not made a public announcement. Still, it was no great secret."

"Could it be a spy or infiltrator?"

"No one wants to say so, but some of us believe it is someone in the group, maybe not the core group, but the larger one. Big corporations don't send little notes saying, *Drop this cause or you'll be sorry.* They have lawyers, and money to bribe the politicians. Why would they strangle a seagull and put it on our boat? It's quite childish, really."

"Have you raised the issue in the core group? At the meeting tonight?"

"No . . ."

"Why not?"

"Because it is so much easier and more usual to see evil outside oneself. Everyone says we must be vigilant, and sooner or later the culprit will reveal himself."

That sounded like a line from *Wie Bitte?* And suddenly I had a dreamlike flash of disaster in a dark harbor, of someone being knocked on the head and thrown into the water. The lesson on indirect objects perhaps.

But as Elke went out the door, I thought, If a child strangled a seagull we would not call it childish. We would find it most disturbing.

The next days fell into a pattern. At seven every morning (Marianne was under the impression because I had arrived on the night train from Paris that I was an early riser, which is far from the truth), Marianne would give a crisp rap to my door and call out, "Breakfast, Cassandra," or alternately, "*Frühstuck*, Cassandra." Since hearing about *Wie Bitte?* she had begun playfully to test my knowledge of German by throwing words into our Spanish and English conversation. The more words I knew the more she threw. "By the end of your visit, we'll be speaking German all the time."

In theory I had the days to myself, in my lovely peaceful room, but Marianne was always knocking and breaking into my thoughts, asking if I wanted more coffee, bringing in little trays with snacks, telling me she was going out shopping—did I want to come and choose my favorite foods, oh yes, it would be amusing, wouldn't it, for me to visit one of the little Turkish shops in the neighborhood, and important too, to meet some Turks face to face, they were having such a hard time in this terrible place, she had experienced it herself, growing up in Santiago among free-spirited Communists and then coming to the university here and having to make her way, having to become more German than the Germans, but, oh, she really shouldn't be interrupting me, and she closed the door softly and apologetically, tip-toeing away. Half an hour later she would be back, wanting to show me an interview with Gloria in a Berlin newspaper or an article in a Chilean journal or a photocopy of a speech Neruda gave from exile. Sometimes the flat would fill with music from her expensive CD player. Stravinksy's *Rite of Spring* was a great favorite of hers.

She was so good-natured and enthusiastic, so clearly pleased to have me as a visitor, that I felt churlish turning down her invitations or pretending I didn't hear her calling me, or even fantasizing about locking my door. Still, when Elke asked me one day if I'd like to go on a local birdwatching expedition, I responded so willingly that she was taken aback. If my friend Lucy Hernandez had been there, she would have been quite surprised. She'd tried for years to put a pair of binoculars in my hands and to explain to me that a robin and a sparrow are not the same thing.

"It's not a serious trip," Elke warned me. "But every month Karin takes a group to one or another of Hamburg's parks and points out local birds and discusses some topic, like nest-building or migratory patterns. It's nice for beginners and for parents with children."

"I'm dying to go," I assured her.

A few hours later I was sitting on a bench with Karin in a park thick with golden-leafed trees while she breast-fed baby Sappho. I had learned the difference between a robin and a sparrow, had even learned their German names. That would show Lucy. The rest of the small group was wandering around a small pond, staring at the ducks and, in the case of the children, feeding them.

"Is Sappho your first?" I asked Karin. In the bright daylight, she looked older than she had at the evening meeting. Well over forty, with gray streaks in her dark hair.

"Yes. Is it so obvious? I keep wanting to pretend to everyone that it's dead easy, though clearly it would have been much easier fifteen years ago! Helmut is even worse, of course. We're trying to share childcare, in the progressive fashion. Which means that each of us is convinced the other doesn't do it quite correctly."

She yawned. The autumn sunlight stopped pleasantly short of being hot, but it was still sleepy-making. "Just last night, in fact," Karin said, "We were having a fight. We were up late discussing this whole business again of the threats to the group. Helmut takes it very seriously. He doesn't want me to take the baby on the demonstration for fear of violence."

"Are you expecting violence?"

"Oh, there's always something with the police," Karin said, shrugging. "I've been in demonstrations over the years where I narrowly escaped being beaten badly. But of course I plan to keep the baby well away from any of that. It's important that we have babies and children at the demonstration. We want to show how destroying the wetlands and bird habitats will affect their future."

"How did the bird-watching go?" Elke asked when I returned. Marianne was mercifully at the university, no doubt lecturing her adoring students about Gloria de los Angeles. Elke poured me a glass of wine, and I sank into one of the huge leather sofas.

"It was wonderful to be outside, out of the house," I said. "Elke, are you expecting violence at the demonstration? A real confrontation with the police?"

"We're not going to instigate it. It may be provoked." She sipped her wine thoughtfully, the sober Bolshevik.

"By the police?"

"Possibly. But to tell you the truth, I'm also a bit worried by a few people in the core group, not the older ones, but Astrid, for instance, that young woman with the tattoos who says so little. She is an environmental scientist and understands a tremendous amount about biological diversity, but other than that I don't know much about her. She is a bit vague about her past."

"I like the DNA spiral up her arm," I admitted, and Elke smiled.

"Well, Astrid did tell me she thought you looked intriguing."

"What about those two men in the leather jackets, Tall and Round?"

"I know them pretty well," Elke said. "The tall one, Peter, I worked with long ago on anti-nuclear issues. He was quite combative then. Sometimes I've wondered if Peter is trying to push our group into a stronger and more aggressive stance. At other times, I think he is very clear-sighted about our difficulties, and that's good."

"And the round one?"

"Until now Kurt hasn't been very politically active. I think he just follows Peter's lead. But he is quite sincere in his interest in birds. He is a very enthusiastic volunteer."

"What about Karin?"

"Karin used to be a heavy-duty politico, but all that's changed now that she's with Helmut. He was never involved in anything during the seventies and eighties, though how that's possible, I don't know."

"Karin said he's nervous about the demonstration."

"I can't imagine him strangling a seagull," Elke said. "He's not that type."

"Could any of them have written those letters?" I persisted. "And why?"

Elke shook her head. "Anyone *could* have done it. Why, I don't know. Maybe someone wants to create a feeling of threat. So that our group will feel more isolated, more fearful, and be easier to manipulate. It's happened before."

I was going to press her further, but the door swung open and Marianne, arms full of papers, books, and groceries, burst in. "Tonight I'm going to make Chilean food," she said radiantly and gave both of us kisses. You really couldn't dislike her. Even though you knew she was going to keep you up half the night.

A week passed, two. I began to suspect that Marianne did not sleep, for I rarely saw her working. She was forever in my room or catching me in long conversations when I was on my way to the bathroom. I wrote to Lucinda that perhaps one should make a new vow: never to stay with strangers just to use their washer-dryers. I wrote to Nicola, hinting that I might be willing to return to London sooner than expected. I wrote to my editor Simon saying the translation was going a little more slowly than I'd planned. On the other hand, my German was improving.

The night watches at *The Juliette* seemed to be having their effect. There had been no more incidents and only one letter, which the birdwatchers had promptly turned over to the press. The media had become quite involved, and everyone was expecting a great deal of publicity for the demonstration on Saturday. All Friday was taken up with preparations, sign-making, phone calls, photocopying of fact sheets.

Friday evening, when Karin called to say that Sappho was under the weather and she wouldn't be able to spend the night on *The Juliette*, I saw my chance. Elke had asked Astrid to substitute. I'd been wanting to see where that DNA spiral ended up.

"Why don't I come too?" I offered.

"What a good idea," said Marianne instantly. "Astrid, Elke, Cassandra, me, we'll all spend the night there. It will be fun, like a party."

We arrived about eleven, Elke in black leather, Marianne in a big quilted jacket and a dozen scarves, and me in some scavenged warm clothes. Astrid was planning to meet us there. There was a thick fog over the river and a smell of oil and fish. The docks were lit, with weak, eerie yellow lamps, but there were few people about. Water slapped against the docks, and intermittently came the hollow blast of a fog horn, lonely and yet warning of danger.

The Juliette looked normal, untampered with, as we unrolled our sleeping bags and lit the lantern. Elke poured us some tea from a Thermos and Marianne chattered.

"Last night I translated the story about the married woman and the servant boy, Cassandra. Isn't it a good one?"

"Is that the one where they couple frenetically or where they frenetically couple?" I said.

Elke laughed and then turned it into a cough.

"I admit," said Marianne without blushing, "that there is a certain amount of heterosexual romance in the stories, but . . ."

"Romance!" said Elke. "It's nothing but soft pornography in the tropics!"

"It's not! It's beautiful writing. Help me, Cassandra. Help me defend Gloria from my unromantic girlfriend."

"It's not beautiful," I mumbled, thinking, Now I have to leave Hamburg by the morning train. I'm glad my clothes are all washed.

"What?" said Marianne. "*Wie bitte?* I didn't hear you."

"What's that noise?" said Elke, sitting bolt upright.

"Where?"

"On the dock, coming down the dock. Is it footsteps?"

"It's just Astrid," said Marianne. "Astrid," she called out, but there was no answer.

The footsteps stopped, not far away. They didn't move away again.

"You'd better call some of the others on the cellular phone," I said.

"Yes." But Elke searched and could not find it. "We must have forgotten it." She took the flashlight and shone it out on the dock. There was not a sound.

"Probably just rats," said Marianne determinedly. "Now, Cassandra, tell me what you were saying. I didn't hear it . . . about Gloria."

"I'm going out to investigate," Elke said.

"No, Elke," said Marianne, but Elke slipped up the short ladder and on to the dock. We saw her light flicker down the dock and then disappear.

"Elke!" Marianne shouted. There was only the sound of the fog horn.

"I'll go see what's happening." I said.

"Don't leave me alone, Cassandra!"

"I'll be back in a second."

I crawled out of the boat on my hands and knees, keeping my flashlight extinguished. I made my way over to the harbor wall and inched along it in the direction that Elke had disappeared. The cement was cold and clammy. The fog was by this time so thick I could see almost nothing. Not even the boat I'd just left.

My nerves were wound to the highest degree, so that when I heard the thump of someone leaping onto the boat, and Marianne's shriek, cut off, I froze and couldn't move. Who was more important for me to save, Elke or Marianne? Let me rephrase that: Who, given the fact that my feet seemed to be stuck to the wet wooden planks of the dock, could I save?

The question soon became more than academic. There was nothing more to be heard from Marianne, except some banging on wood. Had he—she?—shoved her in the tiny water closet? After a few minutes, the boat's engine started. Was he planning to steal the boat with Marianne on it? Was he planning to dump her into the river somewhere?

Adrenaline finally unlocked my knees. I fell forward and started creeping back on my belly over the dock to *The Juliette*. Whoever was driving the boat didn't seem terribly practiced; he maneuvered clumsily away from the berth, knocking against the pilings. As the boat began to pull away, I jumped as quietly as I could into the stern, which was open and had a table and built in seats. I barked my knee sharply on one of the seats.

Limping and crawling, I made my way to the door that connected the back of the boat with the middle sleeping cabin. It was locked. I would have to squeeze around the side of the boat to the pilot's cabin in front. But the boat was hardly stable enough at the moment for any tricky maneuvers. I hung on as the unknown pilot made an ungainly turn away from the other berths, putting us in the direction of the river. I thought of those huge container ships out there somewhere in the fog. This idiot hadn't even put on any lights.

Very faintly, from the dock that had completely disappeared in the thick white mist, I heard feet running and a thin cry, "Marianne! Cassandra!" Well, at least Elke was safe and could get help. Preferably before we sank or were involved in a major collision.

For we were heading out of the inner harbor into the huge, invisible river.

Now it was time to move. I inched as slowly and carefully as I could along the right side of the boat, trying not to look down into what seemed awfully black, cold-looking water. Forward, forward, I thought. Just think forward. Around us there seemed to be nothing but a damp brackish cloud. Finally I squeezed to the right-hand door. How could I possibly get in without being seen? I peeked through the window. No sign of Marianne. At the wheel on the other side of the cabin was a figure all in black, with a ski mask, not exactly a sight to inspire confidence. I thought it was a he, but couldn't tell much more in the shadows. Was it Tall or Round? Was it Astrid?

A fog horn went off somewhere close-by, and I almost lost my balance and toppled into the water. I grabbed the door handle, and it turned and gave, propelling me into the little cabin and straight at the figure at the wheel.

"You will pay for this," I unexpectedly said in German (*Wie Bitte?*'s lesson on future tense maybe?), and grabbed the wheel and gave it a sharp turn. The boat made an abrupt change of direction and the momentum knocked the figure to the other side of the boat, out through the left door, which had swung open in the turn.

I waited for the splash and looked around frantically for the life preserver. Some lighted shape, a buoy I hoped, appeared and disappeared, but not before we ran into it. I struggled to recall my very brief lesson in river piloting from Marianne.

Yes, Marianne. I had to get her out of the toilet, but I was afraid to let go of the wheel. In fact my hands were now frozen fast to the wheel. And meanwhile, where was that life preserver? Where was, in fact, that splash of a human body hitting water?

Out of the corner of my eye I saw a shape clinging to the side of the boat. He—for now he was not just provisionally but actually masculine—had managed not to fall, but to hold on to the left side just as I had on to the right. I couldn't see him well, still, and was afraid to turn my eyes from the window in front of me, though I could see very little in that direction either. He was shouting to me in German.

"Speak English!" I shouted back.

But if he could, his brain was as jammed as mine was, and it wouldn't come out.

I forced myself to remember some basic conversation. "What's your name, please?"

"Helmut."

"Helmut. The father of Sappho?"

"Yes, yes."

"What are you doing?"

But I couldn't understand his response. "*Wie bitte?*" I shouted back, seeing something boat-shaped on the right, and jerking the wheel so that we missed it by inches.

"I only wanted. Only wanted to scare Karin. Not to go to the demonstration. I hate violence."

"What about that seagull?"

"A mistake. I'm sorry."

Should I believe him? My mind said yes, but my instincts were still all wrapped up with that damned television program, once forgotten in my memory bank, now resurrected and imposing itself on reality.

There was the harbor at night. There was a murderer on the loose. There was a boat and a man overboard. There was a chase. There were a lot of people crying, "*Halt! Politzei!*" There was a big crash, and just before the crash had been the Imperative. Watch out for that boat up ahead. Turn! Turn!

What the hell was he saying now? I could barely hear for the banging on the w.c. door behind me. "Hold on, Marianne!" I called, and then to Helmut, "*Wie bitte?*"

"Turn!" he was suddenly screaming in English.

"Well, why didn't you say so in the first place?" I wrenched the wheel around, but not quite quick enough. And that's all I remember for a while.

I had a mild concussion, but the doctor said I didn't have to stay in the hospital long. Bed rest for a week or two and then I should be able to return to normal. Marianne was of course pleased to nurse me. She came into my lovely guestroom every half hour to see how I was doing and to chat. Helmut had been taken into custody but had been released. After his wild ride on the side of the boat, he was only too happy to confess to the officers on the police boat that had caught up with us and that, in fact, I seemed to have run straight into. He'd been worried about Karin as he said. He'd told her he wouldn't be home in time for her to go stay on *The Juliette* with Elke. He thought only Elke would be on the boat and that if he lured her off, he could take *The Juliette* up the river and then sink her somewhere. Not very nice, but it could have been worse. For him, of course, it was worse, because they wanted to charge him with kidnapping and reckless endangerment of life. But the birdwatchers refused to press charges. Their demonstration had gone off splendidly, with only a little healthy bashing here and there, and there was hope for the future that the Elbe wetlands might be saved.

"Of course Karin is not speaking to him at the moment," Marianne reported. "But in the end she'll probably forgive him." She looked wistfully at me from the side of the bed. "If only I hadn't been locked in the toilet. I could have helped you, Cassandra. I could have steered us to safety."

I had been let off with only a very stern warning never *never ever* to attempt to pilot a boat in the Hamburg harbor again.

My punishment was to lie in bed at Marianne's and have her read Gloria de los Angeles to me, first in Spanish, and then, to improve my German, in her translated version. When I got better, however, Astrid took me out one day to the banks of the Elbe and showed me how to identify the birds that lived on the river and in the marshes. I tried to get her to show me the full extent of her tattoos, and finally, in reluctance and pleasure, she did. But the next time I saw her she was with Karin, who had not made up with Helmut after all. They planned to struggle for the ecological revolution and to bring up little Sappho together.

I forgot the difference between a robin and a sparrow.

Days passed. Weeks. One day I got up, as if an alarm clock had rung. I looked in the mirror at my forehead, the bump now turning a mellow jonquil-plum color, and I saw my wasted limbs. And then I took the boat train to London.

The Last Laugh

"We Finns, we are the most depressed people on earth," said the man in the airplane seat next to me. "We are more depressed than the Scandinavians. We are more depressed than the Slavs. That is because Slav and Scandinavian blood runs in our veins together, so the depression is doubled."

"Are you depressed about anything in particular?" I inquired. He was a mere sketch of a man, pale eyes, pale hair, outbrillianced by the cobalt blue of his soccer T-shirt.

"No," he sighed, and looked even more morose. "Just depressed."

"Well," said Luisa Montiflores. She was on my other side on the FinnAir flight from London to Helsinki that was taking us to a writers' conference. "You can't be more depressed than the Uruguayans. We are famous all over South America for our melancholia."

"But you at least have a reason in Uruguay," the Finn argued. "Your politics, your economy, everything like that. While for us, so stable and well-off, it is the human condition in the morning when we wake up that hurts us."

"It's not just a hangover?" I asked, for I recalled that the Finns were serious drinkers. The pale man ignored me. "We're depressed just to wake up and still be alive!" he said.

I got up to use the toilet, and when I returned Luisa had taken my middle seat and the two of them were relating stories of pathology and paralysis, phobia and frenzy, with voluptuous glee. Luisa turned to me only once during the rest of the flight. "But why have I not come to Finland before?" she demanded. "We are made for each other, me and the Finns!"

I'd once had a similar thought years ago, when I spent a weekend in Finland with a young translator I'd met at a conference in St. Petersburg. Helga, who had an arrestingly unpronounceable last name, had invited me back to her family's cabin somewhere north of Helsinki. We ate grilled reindeer steak and potatoes with sour cream, washed down with vodka, and spent most of our time in the wood-fired sauna. Helga could stay in forever, but I was always having to dash out into the snowy drifts. Occasionally she ran out too; she had the longest legs I'd ever seen, and a jubilant laugh as she leapt into the snow. For a while afterward we'd written, but then I'd lost contact with her until a printed wedding announcement with no personal message came in the mail. That must have been eight years ago. I'd heard nothing of her until Luisa showed me the conference brochure. Helga was one of the main organizers.

It was long-legged Helga who was at the gate to meet us, tall as ever and even more beautiful, though far more subdued. She held out her hand to me, but her cool blue eyes betrayed nothing, even though she said formally, "Pleasant to see you again, Cassandra."

"You already know each other?" asked Luisa.

"Another conference years ago," murmured Helga. "In what was then Leningrad. We'll have to catch up sometime. But now we have to hurry. We'll be getting to your hotel just in time to catch a bus with the other participants for the place where your conference is being held. It's by a lovely lake north of the city."

This prestigious writers' reunion had taken place every two years since the early sixties, when Finland had created it to establish dialogue between East and West. Once it had been famous for the drunken Russians speechifying about God and morality and their Western male counterparts trying to keep up with the toasts and saying that they wished someone in their country cared enough about *their* writing to put *them* in the Gulag. But with the end of the Cold War, the organizers had tried to bring in new blood. They cut back on the Bulgarians and invited the feminists, among them Luisa Montiflores and her translator (Luisa always asked for one, on principle, though her English, except in extreme moments, was quite good), Cassandra Reilly.

Luisa loved a junket, but she had another motive for wanting to attend. She knew that the Venezuelan writer Gloria de los Angeles had been invited to the conference two years before, and since then she herself had been angling for an invitation. Her rivalry with Gloria was ludicrous, given that the Venezuelan's magic realism novels had sold in the millions in twenty languages, while Luisa had only been translated into French and English and languished on the backlists of prestigious and impecunious literary publishers. It is the contrary nature, however, of those who write hermetic texts that only postmodern scholars can fully decipher, to long for an enthusiastic public response at the same time as they take pride in their obscurity.

Whatever Gloria had, Luisa wanted, too, but she did not want to hear Gloria's name mentioned, and it was like poison to her when Helga politely said to her in the taxi, "And do you know Gloria de los Angeles? She was here two years ago and made such a sensation. So elegant and witty and such an amazing writer. What a vivid imagination she has. I adore her books, don't you?"

"Her books are shit," said Luisa briefly, running an indifferent hand through her Romaine Brooks style black hair with the white streak in it. "Pots boiling, no more."

Helga was taken aback, but realizing her gaffe—this was neutral Finland, after all—she said, "I certainly can agree with you about her last collection. It was so . . . predictable, really . . . it had nothing new to say. Not like your fiction, Luisa, which is so . . . challenging . . ."

And Luisa unbent slightly to say, "I will autograph my latest book for you." Luisa pulled out a copy of *Saturn's Children*. "Whom shall I inscribe it to?"

"To Helga . . . and Pekka," Helga said, avoiding my eyes. "My husband is a literary critic and admires your work. He'll be so pleased."

The next morning I woke up in the hotel room I was sharing with Luisa to find light streaming across my face. It was only four a.m., however, and I had only gone to bed, in a pearly blue light, three hours ago. I stared out the window at the lake, which was shimmering brightly. Beside it on the shore was an old-fashioned wooden sauna, like Helga's family's.

At the cocktail party the night before, Helga had come in with her husband, this Pekka. He was certainly good-looking, in a sardonic way, but much shorter than she. His long dark hair was pulled back in a ponytail, and he wore a white shirt and black jacket and black jeans. His English was pure SoHo-Manhattan. Helga kept him away from me, so I didn't meet him, but she couldn't keep him away from the rest of the women there, particularly if they were young or wearing décolleté. Helga had the choice of standing awkwardly by his side as he flirted, or removing herself to the other side of the room where, with some dignity, she could pretend to be involved in other conversations while watching him all the time. He didn't care if she watched him. He smoked and he drank, quite a bit, and toward the end of the evening, he pawed. At one point I saw him stroking the round little posterior of a young Dutch writer, who was herself fairly inebriated. Her name tag said she was Marion van Gelder. She had bleached hair about a knuckle-length long and multiply-pierced ears. I thought I saw a contemptuous look in her eye, but she didn't try to stop Pekka. Fortunately Helga seemed to have left by then.

In the morning light, I looked out at the lake; and I looked at Luisa, who, for all her much-publicized angst, had never enjoyed anything but a very good night's sleep ("But my dreams! Absolutely nightmares. Every night, Cassandra."), and who was snoring peacefully. Then I rooted around in my bag and found my notebook. "Finland," I wrote. "Saunas. Reindeer steak. Depression. Midnight sun."

I had another, unannounced reason for wanting to come to Finland. Luisa with her notions of high art, and her family's wealth, would be surprised to find out that in spite of my best intentions, I occasionally thought about money, or my lack of it. The fact is that the career of literary translator into English isn't especially lucrative. Very rarely do any of us manage a small percentage of the royalties; our fees are based on the number of words in a text. In many European countries, literary translation is a respected occupation that provides a steady income. My colleague in Germany, Marianne Schnackenbusch, for instance, constantly has work. But this isn't true in the English-speaking world, at least as concerns literature. There is more work in technical areas, and I'd done plenty of it, but I found it mind-numbing in general.

Thus, I hadn't been adverse to the suggestion made by an American journalist I'd met by chance in Romania a few years ago that we collaborate on a series of travel pieces. Or, as Mr. Archie Snapp wrote when he suggested the idea: "You do the leg work, Cass, and set the scene; I'll rewrite for the public." Archie's public was primarily in the Midwest, beginning with his own local paper in Ann Arbor, *The Washtenaw Weekly Gleaner,* but we (he) had been successful in placing some of our pieces in larger newspapers on occasion.

In Archie's hands, topics like "Revisiting the Paris of the Modernists" had become "Shakespeare and Co.—The Tradition Continues," and my article on the archeological museum of Mexico City had turned into "From Olmec to Aztec, or How Hot Chocolate Was Invented." I let Archie provide the titles and rewrite my sentences. And with no problem at all did I let him take the credit and the byline. All I did was provide him with three to five pages of notes and a few angles, and sometimes a roll of film. And I got half the check. Archie was honest as salt and very reliable. But so far I'd had more disillusion in Finland than inspiration. Every time I wrote *sauna,* I thought of Helga and her obvious unhappiness. I'm used to women lovers getting married; but I like them to marry nice men.

Besides, I wanted some coffee, and breakfast wasn't until eight. I got back in bed with my notebook and soon was fast asleep again.

✈

When I woke up next, it was ten o'clock and Luisa was gone. The first seminar must have already started. I rushed downstairs and ran into Helga, who was carrying a microphone and looking distracted.

"Listen Helga," I said, "about this husband of yours," but she rushed on, explaining, "I *told* the other organizers that the 'Writer and Gender' group would be the biggest, but they said only a few women would want to attend that, that everyone else would want to go to the 'Writer and History' and the 'Writer and the Imagination.' But the 'Writer and Gender' group overflowed the little balcony they assigned them, and we have had to put them under that oak tree. There are so many we need a microphone."

I followed her across the lawn to a group of about thirty people, mostly women, sitting cross-legged in a circle. The discussion was in full swing:

"You can say that because you come from a country like Holland," a woman whose name tag said she was Simone from Algeria was saying vehemently. "I tried to write about myself as a sexual being and what happens? I sell 60,000 copies of my book, but my publisher's life is threatened, there is a public burning, and I end up having to live in Paris."

"I know about notoriety and stigma," the Dutch woman shot back. It was Marion, whom Pekka had flirted with so heavily. She was one of the youngest women there, in her late twenties, and this morning was wearing a skirt and a vest with nothing underneath. Several blue tattoos were visible. "The Dutch pride themselves on their tolerance about prostitution, but they didn't want to hear the true story of my life as a fifteen-year-old call-girl to wealthy men. I too became famous, in the wrong way."

Mayumi, a Japanese woman in her fifties, with a frizzy gray permanent and a no-nonsense air, spoke up. I recognized her as one of Japan's best known writers. "What I wrote in the sixties was regarded as pornography, in the seventies as erotica, and in the eighties as literature. We must have faith in our literary intent, and in ourselves, no matter what they say about us."

"The worst censorship," Luisa said flatly, "is the censorship we perform on ourselves." And she, normally so arrogant and convoluted when she spoke of her work, began to tell a simple and wrenching story about her mother finding her journal when she was fourteen, a journal where she'd written the story of falling in love with another girl.

When she lost her words in English, I took over for her. "That is when I first learned that writing is dangerous. After that I wrote my diary in code. I have written my novels that way too."

The few men in the group had said little up to that point, but now one spoke. He was a tall Finn with little round glasses like John Lennon and floppy hair, younger than the woman he sat next to, who had been clenching her hands until they were almost white. "It is important to recognize that there are other ways to silence a woman writing about sexuality than banning her or her books, or threatening exposure or punishment. Ridicule is an effective silencer, too, and in a small country like Finland, which prides itself on equality, ridicule is perhaps the best weapon there is."

This unleashed a torrent of stories from the Finnish women in the group. How for all the years that this conference had been going on, they had never been invited to speak or lead a group or participate fully. How the whole thing was controlled by a male literary Mafia who just thought of it as a place to get drunk and screw around and play soccer.

"Soccer?" I couldn't help asking.

For this, more than anything, seemed to enrage them most. That every time this conference was held, the men writers played a midnight game of soccer, what Europeans and most of the world besides North America calls *football*.

It was one of the things the conference was famous for, and it was always written about as if it were a great institution: "Finland Against the Rest of the World." But, strangely enough, it always seemed to be Finnish men against men from the rest of the world.

"And if you say anything," said the woman with the clenched hands, "they laugh at you. *But you'd get hurt*, they say. *But women don't like to play soccer*, they say. *But we need you as an audience*, they say. *But why are you making such a big deal about nothing*, they say."

"If nothing else, we must make sure not to be their audience," the Danish poet Birgit said, speaking precisely. "We will organize an evening of our own, perhaps a sauna together down by the lake in the old sauna house."

And the decision, in high good spirits, was made, the women would sauna together, while the men played soccer without an audience. Except for Luisa, who was heard to mutter as she strode off, "I *love* a game of *football*."

But then, Luisa was an unpredictable feminist, to say the least.

Word of our animated seminar got around, and the next day when the group convened again, there were twice as many people. But the self-revelations that had been possible in a smaller group were difficult in a larger one, especially one where there was now a sizable number of men. Some of them were there out of genuine curiosity and some out of prurience. They'd heard the discussion had been about sex, and they wanted to get in on it.

It wasn't that there hadn't been conflict at the first session, but this was disagreement of a different order.

"We can't write explicit sex scenes any more than you can," a British writer called Harold humphed. "If we did, all the women would immediately jump on us for exploiting them."

"So you acknowledge that your so-called sex scene would have to be exploitative then?" the young Dutch writer Marion demanded.

"That's exactly the tone I'm talking about," he said. "I'm in the wrong, aren't I, before I've put pen to paper. It's like trying to write in a police state."

Eva from Prague snorted. "Oh, what in hell do you know about writing in a police state? But I can tell you one thing, since our particular police state ended, there has been nothing but pornography. That's the male idea of freedom—freedom to oppress women."

The debate raged, but as it continued, I noticed something peculiar. The foreign women were talking as much as ever, in the embattled and aggressive manner they'd adopted to defend themselves and that was taken as further evidence of their lack of humor and tolerance; and the men, both foreign and Finnish, had a lot to say (to be fair, their comments were supportive and perplexed, as well as combative). But the Finnish women, so eager to share their stories the day before, were mainly silent. I looked over at the Finnish couple who'd spoken so eloquently—Silje and Tom, I'd heard they were named, the authors and illustrators of a series of children's books—but they didn't add a word to the discussion. From time to time I saw them staring, Silje with nervousness and Tom with real hatred, at a man in the outer circle, Helga's husband Pekka, a man who, as far as I could tell, had said nothing, whose eyes went from one speaker to the next in a curious, amused sort of way. They rested with particular interest on Marion, who was speaking about whores' rights and her own past experience. He didn't stay for the whole session, but wandered off after an hour, hardly acknowledging Helga who had been watching him as intently as he'd been watching Marion.

I caught up with Helga afterward and asked her what had happened, why all the Finnish women were silent.

She paused and said reluctantly, "I would imagine it had something to do with Pekka being there. He writes a literary column for one of the daily papers. He's very well known for his wit. It makes . . . it makes some people afraid of him."

"Are you afraid of him, Helga?" I asked quietly, but she was already moving away, almost running, with that long-legged gait I remembered from years before.

Luisa and I both skipped the afternoon session, and settled down like two asocial cats to work. "Just some memories," she said, when I asked her what she was writing. "And you?"

"A letter to a friend. About Finland."

My articles for Archie often began with some alluring generality about travel that had recently occurred to me. I might be struck one day by what hard work travelling was and how useless that work was. What good to me were the long hours I'd put in reading bus and train and ferry timeta-bles? In my memory, and in the stories I told, my travels seemed composed of an endless succession of peak experi-ences. But in reality, most of what one calls travel is its very opposite—waiting, not moving.

When I tried to put some of my evanescent thoughts down, to capture the subtle sense of working hard and often to little apparent purpose, only to have a fleeting impression of something deliciously bizarre or magnificently ordinary, Archie reduced my carefully honed words to variations on standard clichés: "Travel is ten percent inspiration and ninety percent perspiration," he might begin, continuing, "but don't let that put you off! A few simple tips [I had of course not offered any tips, only bittersweet reflections] can help make your trip an easier one, and give you more time to enjoy the peak experiences that make travel such a memo-rable and rewarding activity."

Sitting on my bed in front of the view of the lake (Luisa had commandeered the desk and chair), I clutched at elusive images of fire and ice, overpowering heat and frigid winds, lakes and fires and the midnight sun. All the time knowing that by the time my story appeared in the *Washtenaw Weekly Gleaner* it would probably be titled "Sauna Like It Hot" and begin: "Winter or summer Finland calls to the adventurous tourist. But whether you're skiing, or biking, or swimming in one of Finland's many lakes, you can relax at the end of the day in the dry heat of a pine-scented sauna. *Sauna* is, after all, a Finnish word."

Late that night, the midnight soccer game took place on a grassy meadow near the hotel, but as promised many of the women didn't attend, instead gathering at the old sauna house on the lake. Luisa had still been writing when I left her. It was something to do with the story she'd told the day before about her mother finding her journal. The shouts and screams of the soccer players and their audience floated across the grounds and down to the lake, but very faintly. When we went into the sauna, we couldn't hear them at all. The group was a handful of Finnish women and six foreigners—Mayumi, Simone, Marion, Eva, Birgit, and me. All of us foreigners had to leave the hot sauna before the natives. Naked, we ran outside and plunged into the lake. Male laughter wafted down to us, and Simone shuddered as she rose out of the water and headed back to the sauna.

"It's strange being naked like this out in the middle of nowhere," she said. "Frightening, but liberating somehow. I want to do it. Yet I keep looking over my shoulder."

Marion said, "I made a resolve when I was young that I would never be afraid of anything, I would never let a man stop me from doing anything."

"You sound like my daughter," Birgit said. "I admire that. She tells me stories of travelling in foreign places, how she threatened a man who tried to rape her with a knife. I wasn't brought up like that."

"I hate to hear the sound of men laughing in a group," Simone began, and then stopped. "Well, that's all over now. I can never go back while the fundamentalists have so much power. My sister and her husband and children have left too, we all live together in Paris now, and perhaps forever."

We spent several hours at the lake. Mayumi and Birgit managed to stay in the longest, while Eva, Marion, Simone and I opted for briefer and briefer visits to the sweltering sauna and spent increasing amounts of time chatting on the dock. The Finnish women left together, then Eva and Simone, and then Birgit. I told Mayumi and Marion that I was starting to feel like a plate of salmon mousse and would have to leave.

As I walked back across the grounds to my room in the hotel, I could hear the sounds of drunken male laughter. It sounded like the game was winding up. I thought of what Simone had said and shuddered slightly. I put a bold face on, but I never felt completely, totally safe anywhere alone at night, and I, like Simone, did not like the sound of men laughing in a group. Perhaps to humanize them again, I walked over to the lit field, just in time to see a familiar figure knock the hurtling ball away from the goal with her elegant forehead.

A cheer went up and Luisa was mobbed. The Finns had lost, the Rest of the World, Including One Woman, had triumphed. There was always this alternative to boycotting segregated pleasures, wasn't there? To take part anyway as the spirit moved you and show them that you were as good as or better than they were.

And who was to say which way was best? Certainly at that moment my own tomboy youth came back to me and I wished I had been in the game to kick the ball past Luisa, rather than sitting in the all-girl's clubhouse, feeling superior, envious, and just a little bit afraid.

The next morning at breakfast word flew through the room: Pekka had been found in the sauna by himself, dead of a heart attack. No one remembered seeing him go into the sauna; the last time anyone remembered seeing him was in the confusion at the end of the game.

The last people to have the key to the sauna that night were the women, including we six foreigners who had stayed latest.

"I don't know how he could have gotten in there," said a shaken Marion over coffee. "I know I was the last person to use the sauna, but I locked it up after I left and put the key back in the office. I didn't give the key to anyone. It was too late. There must be another key."

According to the hotel staff, there wasn't, and the key that Marion said she had replaced in the office was not there. It had been found in the sauna door. Pekka could have removed it, but it was unlikely he could have locked himself in. Hearing this news, we began to understand that Pekka hadn't just died naturally of a heart attack.

But it wasn't until the Finnish police showed up an hour later and asked us six women who'd been in the sauna that evening to make statements that we realized they definitely thought Pekka had been murdered, and possibly murdered by one of us.

Only real murderers live their lives with a good alibi. The rest of us sound guilty as sin and have no excuses for anything. When interrogated, no one has seen us, no one has heard us. We could have been up to anything. Although Eva and Simone had left together, the rest of us had departed separately and walked back to the hotel alone. Birgit had stopped briefly to chat with a Norwegian writer, and Simone had been seen on the phone in the lobby; the rest of us had apparently been invisible. We didn't even have the excuse that our movements had been hidden in the dark.

It's not a pleasant thing to be suspected of a murder, and none of us felt very happy about it. True, the immediate headlines would be in Finnish, which none of us could read, but eventually they would be picked up other places: "Battle of the Sexes Turns Fatal in Finland."

I had just come out of my session with the police, who, in spite of their cool Scandinavian politeness, were as suspicious as any cops I'd ever come across. "And where, exactly, do you live, Mrs. Reilly? Ah, *nowhere just at the moment*? Nowhere? And is that possible, Mrs. Reilly? To live *nowhere just at the moment*?"

I saw the Finnish couple, Silje and Tom, slowly crossing the lawn, and rushed after them.

145

"Tell me about this man Pekka," I said. "Who was he? I should at least have an idea about someone I'm supposed to have possibly murdered."

They looked at each other and motioned to a bench nearby. It was Silje who spoke, in careful English and without affect. Her husband Tom looked more upset than she did.

"It was about ten years ago," she said. "I was quite young, twenty-two. I had just written my first novel. It was very graphic, sexually graphic. I thought it might be shocking, but at the time I thought I wanted to shock. I had been living in France, studying, and took French writers as my models. I wrote frankly about incest, bisexuality, a woman who is sexually used by an older man, but who also finds pleasure in it. I wrote about masochism. I believed the world needed to know all this. I was something like the Dutch woman Marion, only not so experienced and brave."

She stopped and, tears choking her voice, couldn't go on.

Tom took her hand. "The novel became famous. It *was* shocking. But also very strong, very beautifully written. It had no easy answers. It was only a woman's voice, telling the truth. There were people who didn't like to hear a woman's voice. What I said two days ago, in the group, about ridicule. That's the weapon they chose."

"When you're young, you don't expect to be laughed at," Silje broke in, more forceful now. "It's really the worst insult, not to be taken seriously. This man, this Pekka, that's what he did. He wrote about me, not my book, about me. He interviewed friends and my family, found out I'd stayed once in a mental institution, that I'd used drugs. Everything he found out he used against me, and trivialized me and made it sound like I'd made everything up. That I was just a silly little, attention-seeking fool. After that article came out, I was so ashamed."

She swallowed. "I tried to kill myself and failed. I was committed to an institution for almost two years."

Tom took over again. "Silje and I have tried to live a quiet life the past few years. We do our children's books. We now have two children of our own. We live in the country and don't participate in the writers' debates in Helsinki. But when the invitation came to attend this reunion, we said, All right, why not? After all we too are part of Finnish literature.

"All last evening and night I thought about what the newspaper would say this morning about the discussion. How he would make fun of all the writers, the men as well as the women, but especially the women. How he would laugh at the Japanese woman for being over fifty now and well-known for her erotica, how he would turn that girl Marion into a call-girl again.

"How he would laugh at Silje and me being there," Tom said, "—'the two children's writers getting an earful.'"

"We couldn't let the article come out," said Silje.

"But how do you know what he'd written?"

"We didn't know," said Tom quickly, pulling at Silje's arm.

"We only suspected," Silje said, but her eyes didn't quite meet mine.

I changed the subject. "How did Helga marry a guy like that?"

Tom shook his head. "I knew her from years ago. She was a friend of my sister's. She was very wild and free. I think she was a challenge to him. So he decided to break her. He sleeps with everyone he can. Almost right in front of her."

I remembered how he'd touched Marion's arm at the cocktail party, and how she'd let him. How did that fit with the fact that Marion had been the last in the sauna? She had insisted on staying while the rest of us staggered away. She was a strange combination: punk and tough with a little bit of sex kitten. Had she arranged to meet him there? I didn't want to think that.

I wanted Luisa's advice, but she was holed up in our room, writing away and wouldn't open up. "It's sad, it's very depressing, my life," she shouted through the keyhole in jubilation. "I have to write it. I shall not stop until I write it all down."

"But Luisa, everything is in an uproar. A man is dead. They think he might have been murdered. You can't just stay in there and write!"

There was a silence and then she came to the door. "Who died?"

"Pekka, the literary critic. Helga's husband."

"But he told me he likes my work."

"That's no guarantee against murder."

"Cassandra, I hope it wasn't you," Luisa scolded. "Some women just aren't cut out to be lesbians. You must accept that and not murder their husbands."

"Of course I didn't kill him."

"Well, he did have a very unpleasant laugh," Luisa remarked, before locking me out of the room again.

Out on the lawn a struggle was in progress. Two plainclothes Finnish detectives were on either side of Marion, dragging her unwillingly to their car. They had gotten her confession, the word went around the group of writers standing shocked on the grass, that Pekka had accosted her in the sauna when she'd been there alone, and that she'd escaped and locked him in to die of overheating.

"We can't let this happen," said Simone. "There must be more to the story. We must protest."

"I should never have let Marion stay there alone," said Mayumi. "I said to her, 'Come with me, Marion, don't stay here alone,' and she said, 'No, I'm fine. Just ten more minutes.'"

And then the police car was gone. Now for the first time I saw Helga. She was standing under a tree, watching the whole scene from a distance.

"I'm so sorry," I said, going over to her.

"Don't be. Whatever Marion did to him, he probably deserved."

"You're sure she did something?" I said, taken aback at Helga's harsh tone. She looked years older this morning, her blonde hair slicked back, her skin pale and clammy.

"She came to me early this morning and told me about it. How he found her in the sauna alone after all the rest of you had left. He was drunk, she said. He tried to attack her, but she easily got away from him and locked the door. She only meant to teach him a lesson."

"But when she went back to let him out, he was dead?"

"Exactly. It only took a short while. She didn't realize he had a heart condition."

"But that's not really murder, then." I was relieved.

"That's what I told the police." Helga looked at me. "That I didn't think she meant to kill him."

"You went to the police then?"

"Yes, I told them. I couldn't cover it up for her."

Her iciness puzzled me. She may no longer have loved Pekka, but could she be glad that he was dead? Perhaps it was suppressed anger that made her seem so remote and hard.

"Please excuse me. There are many things to arrange. Under the circumstances, I don't know if the conference will be continuing," she said, and started across the lawn to the main offices.

I watched her walk away with those long legs that had once leaped over the snowbanks. "I like the sauna to be as hot as possible," she'd told me that weekend long ago. "As hot as would kill most people."

The conference was declared over and hasty preparations begun to transport us all back to Helsinki. If I didn't work fast, I might lose my opportunity. I found Silje and Tom getting into a car in the parking lot.

"May I just ask you a couple of questions before you go?"

They said nothing, so I asked anyway. "Was it generally known that Pekka had a heart condition?"

They shook their heads. "Perhaps among his friends. We didn't know."

Silje was already sliding into the driver's seat when I asked, "Would you be willing to turn over the article that Pekka wrote to the police?"

149

"But how?" she began and Tom interrupted, "We never saw any article. We only imagined what it would have in it." He got in the passenger seat and slammed the door.

Seconds later they were gone.

The rest of us were given two hours to pack up and meet back at the bus. In a small group, the women from the sauna huddled together. Because none of us thought that Marion had killed him on purpose, the question was complicated. Had Marion been framed, or had it merely been an impetuous response to Pekka's unwelcome overtures? Birgit said she was bound to get off. Mayumi remembered a similar case in Japan, a murder that had been made to look like a suicide. Eva hinted at conspiracy, and Simone quickly joined her in wondering whether larger forces had not been involved. It was only on the bus, when I was sitting next to Luisa, that I thought to ask her when she'd had a chance to hear Pekka's laugh, the laugh she said was so unpleasant.

"After the football game. He was in a group, laughing, I think with some Finns, that young pair of children's authors. And Helga. Then the Finns walked off, looking angry. And he came by with Helga to congratulate me on heading off the goal ball. We talked about my work, and then the two of them walked away."

"In what direction?"

"I don't remember. The office, I think. He had some papers in his hands."

"Was he drunk?"

"Yes, a bit. Helga was holding his arm. He was laughing."

"What time was this?"

"Oh, quite late. Or perhaps very early."

The conference by the lake might be over and the Finnish writers dispersed back home, but the foreign participants still had several days to wait for our return flights. Only Birgit, for family reasons, showed an interest in getting home sooner. She changed her ticket and left shortly after our bus arrived in Helsinki. The rest of us—Mayumi, Eva, Simone, and me—checked back into a central hotel. Luisa, in her inimitable way, had actually rented a flat in the city so as not to disturb her writing process. She would stay in Finland until *Diary of a First Love in Montevideo* was finished.

She urged me to come stay with her, but I felt too unsettled to take her up on it. I did make some cursory excursions around Helsinki, scribbling my final notes for Archie, describing with many adjectives the colorful market by the harbor, the splendid Russian orthodox church, the impressive monument to Sibelius, the fascinating outdoor museum with its authentic farm and country buildings. However mostly I spent hours with my new friends, discussing what had happened to Pekka and how we might help Marion.

Helga seemed to have vanished. I had no easy way of contacting Silje and Tom. All three of them, it seemed to me, had far greater motives—longer-standing motives certainly—for killing Pekka than Marion had. In the end, it was to Mayumi that I shared my suspicions and the little information I had, for Eva and Simone, with their experience of state repression, consistently drifted into conspiracy theories. Pekka was a journalist, wasn't he, and in Czechoslovakia and Algeria journalists who were on to something were often threatened or kidnapped or outright murdered. Pekka could have been killed by government agents who then pinned it on Marion.

It after one of these sessions with Eva and Simone, at breakfast on the morning after we returned from the lake, that Mayumi caught up to me in the lobby as I was going out to send my Finnish observations to Archie, and suggested that after the post office we stop by the newspaper where Pekka had worked.

This was the *Helgosin Sanomat*, which sounded more like a particularly tidy launderette than a newspaper, but it was Helsinki's largest daily. We asked to see Pekka's editor and his assistant came out to the lobby to escort us up. To my surprise, the assistant was none other than the depressed young man from the FinnAir flight.

He recognized me too. "And your friend Luisa Monti-flores?"

"She's staying on in Helsinki for a while, writing," I said. "She says Finland is like a television movie with the sound turned very low."

The meeting with the cultural editor was brief and not very useful. He was a balding man with darting eyes in an immobile face. He shrugged away our concern that Pekka might have been murdered by someone who didn't like what Pekka was planning to write or had written about them.

"Ladies, the late Pekka wrote many articles over many years that poked fun at many writers. If someone was going to kill him, they had ample reason before now."

"Do you have the article he was writing at the lake, about the conference?" Mayumi asked him point blank.

"I don't see what his article has to do with anything," the editor blustered. "No one has asked to see it, and besides, we don't have it. *I've* never seen it, anyway."

"And that's that," said Mayumi, as we were shown out. We sat down on some modern looking chairs in the lobby, unsure what to try next.

"There are several questions I ask myself," said Mayumi, and I recalled I had read in her biographical notes that she had an advanced degree in psychology. "First, obviously: who had a reason to kill him? Someone he had harmed, or was about to harm.

"Second, what was that reason? Was it fear, or was it revenge? The former suggests an uncalculated, perhaps hasty response. The latter a more premeditated plan.

"Then, I'm curious about two more things. Who knew that locking Pekka in a very hot sauna might kill him? That is, who knew he had a heart condition? And finally, why kill him at such a public event, where the chances of being discovered or seen were very great?"

"But where the possibilities of pinning the blame on someone completely outside Pekka's usual circle were very great, too," I reminded her.

We sat staring at each other for a moment. I had earlier dismissed Mayumi, I blush to say, as a grandmotherly type: gray perm, glasses, a pantsuit and scarf. Suddenly I realized that in spite of my bomber jacket and black jeans, my hair was also gray and I could only be a few years younger than she, at most.

I also remembered, with a jolt, a few tasty passages from one of her novels, a scene between two women.

Behind the glasses were curious, warm black eyes. Her skin was ivory and smooth.

"Intimacy. Humiliation. Revenge. Exquisite organizational skills. The ability to dissimulate," Mayumi said. "All these were necessary."

We were interrupted by the pale and breathless assistant, who came skidding to a halt in front of us. "You're still here," he said. "I thought I would have to track you down at your hotel."

He was holding two sheets of paper, copied from a fax. "The editor was not quite telling the truth," he said. "Pekka's article came in the middle of the night. I don't have time to translate it for you, but I can tell you what's in it. It was never published."

"Why didn't the editor run it?" Mayumi asked.

"He didn't think it came from Pekka. He didn't think Pekka wrote it."

"Why not?"

The assistant looked bewildered. "It's an apology," he said. "To all the writers he had mocked over the years."

On my way to Helga's apartment, I thought of what Mayumi had said: "Intimacy. Humiliation. Revenge. Exquisite organizational skills. The ability to dissimulate."

There could be no one but Helga. All that remained was to put together some coherent time frame for the actual murder, between the last time anyone had seen them, well after midnight, and the time the fax had arrived at the newspaper office. The article of course was written by Helga. I should have left it to the police, of course, but I couldn't bear to let her go out of my life without seeing her again.

The assistant had given me her address. It was in a quiet block of tall, nineteenth-century terraced houses, all painted white and sparkling in a sunshine so constant it was beginning almost to grate on me.

Behind her door, I felt her regarding me through the peephole. Then she let me in.

She was in a summer suit, a light blue that matched her eyes. Her hair was pale as whipped honey, and her skin quite brown. She did not look relaxed, but she didn't look agitated either. I noticed that a cotton coat was thrown over a suitcase in the hall. I remembered the first time I'd ever seen her, in Leningrad, at a dismal gathering at one of the Intourist ballrooms. She had been only twenty-five then, gangly in an ill-fitting skirt and jacket, her idea of what a professional woman travelling abroad should wear. Actually I'd heard her before I'd seen her that evening. She was laughing. A joyous, dithery laugh that came from deep inside.

I hadn't heard her laugh once this time.

"I know about the article you wrote in Pekka's name. The apology."

Without answering, Helga led me to a couch in the middle of the room. The flat had tall ceilings and was starkly furnished. Perhaps it was this starkness that gave me the feeling she was packing up and leaving permanently. The tall drapes were drawn, as if Helga too found the constant light tiring.

I noticed a pile of photographs on the wooden coffee table between us. They were turned over, and a few had words on the back. As if Helga had been sorting them or filing them when I came.

Helga clearly wasn't talking, so I decided to get on with it. "I thought at first it might be Silje and Tom who wrote the article of apology, since they seemed somehow to know

154

about another article, perhaps the one Pekka really wrote. But I somehow doubt that if they'd killed him, they could have been cool enough to send a fax afterward. They didn't easily have access to the office. They didn't know Pekka's style of writing. Most important, they seem to lack sang-froid. It's hard for them to hide their feelings."

"I wanted Pekka to go out not as hated as he had been," said Helga softly. "It's a shame the newspaper never printed it."

"So you admit you wrote the apology. Did you also lock him in the sauna?"

She was cool as ice. "Why don't you think Marion did it?"

"Because Marion wouldn't lie."

"I think you have too high an opinion of her," Helga said. She reached between us to the table and began to turn over the photographs. "I just had these developed. They're a little murky, but I didn't want to use a flash. Fortunately it was still light enough after midnight to get a decent picture. Well, perhaps decent is the wrong word."

The snapshots showed a man and a woman in a variety of graphic sexual positions. The sauna was in the background. They were on and around a bench set slightly back in the birch trees. None of the positions looked coerced. Marion's blond head was easy to make out; so was Pekka's black ponytail.

"Pekka's excuse was that he was drunk, of course," said Helga rather tiredly. "It often was."

"Did you confront them?"

"No. I saw him go into the sauna after Marion had left. I saw him open it with the key she'd given him. He left the key in the lock."

She stopped, and I knew this was the nearest she'd get to admitting she had turned the key herself. She seemed flattened, dream-like, almost ghostly in the darkened room. A sliver of hot brightness outlined the windows, but inside all was dim.

"Was it the next morning you told Marion you had photographs?" I asked, as if I were just making conversation.

"We talked. She realized I knew she'd had sex with my husband."

"She didn't know he'd been murdered at that point, I would imagine," I went on, as casually as before. "I suspect she tried to play on your sympathies by telling you he'd forced her to have sex with him. You pretended to believe her and then you told the police she'd confessed it all to you. She was trapped at that point."

"I think she'll get off if she sticks to her story," said Helga dispassionately. She began to put the photographs back into their envelope. "I don't plan to show the photographs to anyone unless I have to. The little slut," she said suddenly, and her eyes flashed. "But then, he always had that effect on women. You wanted to despise him; you thought you did despise him. And yet you found him attractive and compelling all the same."

It was eerie how calm she was again. "I still don't understand some things," I said. "Luisa told me she saw you and Pekka leave the playing field together, and that he was laughing."

"Yes, he had given a copy of his article about the conference to Silje and Tom, just to torment them. Then he wanted to fax it. We went to the office together. I read it and was horrified. I persuaded Pekka to let me fix some typos and so on. I said I'd fax it. He said fine; he was really quite drunk. He wandered away. I didn't fax his article. I ripped it up. When I went back to our room, he wasn't there. That's when I went looking for him."

"And the camera?"

"I've had a camera in my pocket the whole conference," she said without amusement. "For the fun, candid shots I was supposed to be taking."

"Are you sorry?"

"That he's dead? I don't know the answer to that yet."

"You're not planning to flee the country?" I gestured to the suitcase.

156

"What a thought!" For the first time Helga seemed to wake up a little. "No, I'm going to that little house in the country that my grandparents built. That one you and I went to once, all those years ago. If you want to tell the police anything I've told you, go ahead. I'll be there."

She didn't know what I'd do, I realized. And neither did I. When I told Mayumi later, I said, "Let's wait and see what happens to Marion first. If she's really in danger . . ."

"You're loyal to your lovers, I can see," said Mayumi.

"I used to think that feminism made us loyal to each other," I said. "It's still my fantasy."

"Tell me about your fantasies."

"Turn off the light first."

Weeks later, I heard from Luisa, who had finally left Finland, that the charges against Marion had been dropped. The prosecutor's office found no evidence of malicious intent. Pekka was a womanizer, it was well known. He had tried to force Marion against her will; she had responded by locking him in the sauna. She hadn't known of his heart condition.

Luisa also sent along an article about herself written by the new literary critic at the *Sanomat,* our pale depressed friend from the FinnAir flight. Of course it was in Finnish, but Luisa assured me it was nothing but praise. Her favorite kind of critical review.

Both the clipping and the letter came to me in a parcel otherwise filled with Luisa's new novel in manuscript, *Diary of a First Love in Montevideo.* They were delivered to me at Mayumi's old wooden house in Kyoto, where I have been for several months, gathering travel notes for Archie's articles and practicing positions more graphic than anything Marion and Pekka ever tried.

I will set to work translating immediately. Nothing in Luisa's novel corresponds to the truth of her life as I know it. But it is still an extraordinarily cool and melancholy account of love thwarted, shamed and, finally, destroyed.

The Antikvaariat Sophie

"Abby's dead?"

Around me the conversation stopped. My friend Eloise had handed me the phone in the middle of a dinner to welcome our mutual friend Joke, the Human Pretzel, back to Holland. Joke had just returned from a year in Beijing studying advanced acrobatics.

"Abby can't be dead."

Rachel, Abby's lover, had tracked me down in Amsterdam, where I was taking a break from the English winter. Not that it's any warmer in Amsterdam but the Dutch seem to know how to get through the cold wet season in a cozier fashion. Now she was telling me the gruesome details and asking me to come help her sort out papers.

"Yes, of course I'll come to Brussels. Tomorrow."

"Your friend Abby from London?" asked Eloise. It was Eloise's dinner table and Eloise's flat in the hotel she managed near the Vondel Park. Long ago she'd been a Women's Studies professor in the States, but she'd come to Amsterdam to write her novel and had never gone home.

"Yes. She's been living in Brussels for a few years. Was living."

"How'd it happen?" asked Joke. She looked very small across the table; I'd forgotten how small she was, more like a twelve-year-old boy than a thirty-year-old woman, though her white-blonde crewcut and French-striped shirt also helped with the effect.

159

"She was leaving the Gare Midi in Brussels when someone in a hurry drove his car into her. Hit and run. They haven't found him."

It could have happened to anyone. It could have happened to me. I was always dashing across streets without looking properly around me. When Abby and I had been young and in love, we had never paid the slightest attention to traffic. We'd believed ourselves invincible.

"I never look out for where I'm going," said Joke, shaken.

"Me either," said Eloise. She was a slow-moving, dreamy person, the sort you fear might harm herself unintentionally with a sharp object or be mugged in broad daylight.

"Now you, Eloise, I'd worry about," I said, turning back to dessert. "Joke, on the other hand—she'd probably just do a double back flip over the hood of the car."

People in shock often make such flippant remarks. And my friends laughed. Still, none of us could quite finish our apple cake.

Lesbians live in Belgium of course, because lesbians live everywhere. They live alone and they live with friends, and they live with their partners of six years, as Abby had lived with Rachel. It's not illegal to be a lesbian in Belgium, but that's because legally you don't exist. You exist as a taxpayer, and as a worker and consumer participating in the Belgian economy; but as for deciding who should get your money after you're dead, you don't really have a choice. In the eyes of the law you're single, unattached except through blood. Only family members can inherit. And lesbians are never, can never be, family to each other.

"If I had any idea that the will we made wasn't valid in Belgium," Rachel said, "I never would have moved here. We paid a British solicitor to draw it up for us with power-of-attorney, everything. It's useless."

"But surely you could challenge the Belgian law. You're American citizens, you're just in Belgium for . . ." I hesitated.

I had no clear idea why they were in Brussels. I knew that Abby had inherited some money from an aunt of hers about a year ago, and that, without talking much about it, she'd begun to live a very different lifestyle.

"And how would I pay the lawyer?" Rachel said bitterly. "Our money was in a joint account, and that account is now closed. Closed to me anyway. Wide open for Abby's legal heir."

We were in their apartment off the Avenue Louise, a luxurious flat that I'd never been to before. When I first knew Abby in the seventies, she was just another young American in London, squatting in abandoned houses, working for free at the women's bookstore. Her passion even then had been for collecting books and manuscripts, the odd bit of correspondence. She had eventually gotten a job in one of the antiquarian book shops near the British Museum where she specialized in firsts by twentieth-century women authors. Our affair was brief; our friendship had lasted years. We used to get together for cappuccinos on Coptic Street, a tradition that continued after she moved to Belgium last year, because she came back frequently to London. So I'd never seen this Brussels flat before and was suitably impressed.

"Take a good look," said Rachel as she showed me around. "I won't be living here much longer. Abby's brother will be here to take possession tomorrow and unfortunately the security box at the bank, which I'm now barred from opening, has a complete inventory."

"But Rachel, surely he'll let you keep living here. Surely he'll . . ."

I trailed off when I saw the expression on her face. "Abby's family hated the fact that she was a lesbian; that's why she came to London in the first place. Even though her parents are dead, her brother still has the same feelings, plus he was furious that their aunt left her this place. Now's his chance to get it back. Do you think he's going to let me have anything?"

When Abby first got together with Rachel, all her friends had been surprised. Little scruffy, streetwise Abby with her

New York accent, five-foot-two, a mop of unruly brown hair that hid her eyes but not her pugnacious chin. Ratty sweaters, jeans from the boy's department, boots whose rhinestones were mostly gone. How had Abby gone and fallen in love with a Long Island housewife with a shiny black pageboy and a closetful of clothes? Looking now at Rachel, face wrinkled and sagging, eyes red from tears and lack of sleep, black hair shot with white and pulled back into a careless ponytail, I realized she was well over fifty. Rachel had left her husband of twenty-five years for Abby. She'd never had a job outside the home. Her ex-husband wouldn't provide for her, and she had no marketable skills. She'd followed Abby first to London and then to Brussels, and lost contact with whatever community she'd had in Long Island. Now, in addition to losing Abby, she was about to lose her home, her income, and her financial future.

"Not that I especially want to live in Brussels," Rachel said, leading the way to an elaborately carved wooden secretary. "If I knew where to go and what to do, I'd be out of here in a flash."

She stood looking at two framed photos of Abby on the desk. One was of Abby at eight or nine, with missing teeth in a wide grin; the other was of Abby from a few years ago, still tough and impish.

"I didn't ask you to come Brussels just to hold my hand, Cassandra," she said finally. "I thought you might be able to help me figure out what some of these papers might refer to. You knew Abby for a long time; you might have some idea what she was up to in London and Amsterdam."

I looked at the pieces of paper on the desk. Bills of sale, mostly, with the price in pounds or guilders. But what the objects purchased were was somewhat unclear. Not many of the receipts had names at the top. Only a small handful, in fact. A few were printed with the name of a London bookshop on Coptic Street, the one where Abby had once worked, and the others were stamped Antikvaariat Sophie, Keizersgracht, Amsterdam. An antikvaariat is a second-hand bookstore.

"They must be receipts for books that Abby bought," I said.

"I thought that at first myself," said Rachel, "but then I wondered, Where are these books? Abby had been getting rid of her collection over the last six months. She certainly wasn't buying new books."

I looked at the receipts again and calculated the rate of the pound and the guilder. Some were for modest amounts, a few were sizable, and two of the Dutch ones were astronomical. Whatever Abby had bought at the Antikvaariat Sophie, it had cost her many hundreds of dollars.

"I asked myself, Was it drugs?" Rachel said. "But Abby seems the last person to have gotten into drugs."

"Nor do drug dealers usually give receipts."

Rachel dug farther into one of the drawers and came up with an envelope of cash. "I found this too. It's enough to live on for perhaps three months." She held it out to me. "But I want you to use some of it, Cassandra, to help me."

"How?"

"You know Amsterdam, you have friends there"—she sounded wistful—"Could you go to this used bookstore, and find out what Abby was buying? Maybe it's valuable. I can't go myself—I've got to be here when Abby's brother arrives tomorrow."

I opened the envelope. There was more than three months of groceries in there, but then, I'm more frugal than Abby and Rachel had obviously been. "And if it turns out that Abby had something of value that isn't in the inventory, that she didn't even tell you about . . . ?"

"It wouldn't be illegal to withhold that from her brother," Rachel said, and then she laughed grimly. "Listen to me. I'm worried about doing something illegal. After what the Belgian state has done to me."

Brussels is a city on a grand scale. Boulevards and parks, an enormous palace, a beautifully restored central square, nineteenth-century shopping arcades of glass and wrought iron. In spite of all this grandeur, it used to have a kind of blackened shabbiness that I once found appealing. Now, except in pockets, like around the Gare Midi, for instance, all that sad grit and glamour was giving way to the gleam of corporate headquarters and European Community buildings.

Amsterdam may have as much big business as Brussels, but you don't feel it so strongly. The scale is small, the streets and buildings human-sized. You can walk it easily, and it never seems overwhelming. It had begun to rain on my trip back to Amsterdam that afternoon, a thick marine downpour. But it let up as the train pulled into the Central Station, and I decided to head for one of the inner canals, the Keizersgracht, on foot.

The Antikvaariat Sophie was a shop I'd noticed and forgotten on my strolls around the canals. Some of the other bookstores, just as small, had more lively and inviting shopfronts, often with painted wooden signs and bikes out front, often clustered together, in neighborly fashion. The Antikvaariat Sophie had a more solitary look to it, squeezed as it was between tall, narrow residences. It was that solitude more than any shabbiness, any dustiness that gave the bookstore its closed in, secret look.

Not secret perhaps. Private. I remembered Abby, with a force I didn't usually see in her, saying at our last meeting: "Americans don't believe in privacy. If you don't respond to the most prying question, they believe you're holding out on them."

At the time I'd agreed. Long years abroad had given me a great reluctance to discuss my personal affairs with acquaintances, much less on television. But I never made a big deal of it; when effusive Americans demanded to know whom I was seeing and what my plans were, I simply lied. Now I wondered what Abby might have meant when she'd talked about privacy. Who was asking her questions? What secrets had she kept, even from Rachel?

A tiny bell jingled when I opened the door to the Antikvaariat Sophie, and a woman looked up, neither friendly nor unfriendly, from behind a desk piled with papers and books. There were piles of books everywhere, on tables, alongside the shelves, in boxes. Most of them were books by women, everything from battered old copies of *Sisterhood is Powerful* to *The Life of Hildegard von Bingen*. It was a narrow room, with a cozy look. A few framed black-and-white photographs on the wall—I recognized Vita Sackville-West—and a well-worn armchair with a table next to it.

I would have loved to spend an hour or two looking through the shelves, where Audre Lorde's poetry rubbed challengingly up against that of Elizabeth Bishop's, where Lillian Hellman duked it out with Diana Trilling, and Simone de Beauvoir reminisced in fat volumes and Colette in slender ones. Shelves where women at first shyly and then more and more vehemently confessed their deepest feelings. Shelves of political tracts and shelves of oddities. Shelves where I might find first editions of Tommy Price's wonderful old travel books. However, I remembered that I'd told Rachel I'd try to call her this evening with news.

I took out a few receipts and placed them on the cluttered desk in front of the bookseller. She was a compact, solid woman in her forties, dressed in a striped shirt and khaki trousers. She had a shrewd, amused look that was not particular to her but to her countrymen and women. I had often felt the Dutch were having a quiet joke at my expense.

"Ah," she said. "Then something has happened to Abby."

"You knew her then?"

"Knew . . . yes. Oh, yes."

"I'm sorry to tell you—she was killed in a car accident."

"A car accident?"

"Someone in a Fiat hit her outside the Gare Midi two days ago, around five in the afternoon. They didn't stick around."

The solid woman looked down. I couldn't see her expression. "And these?"

"It looks like she had recently been buying books or something from you."

"Books? From me?"

"It says Antikvaariat Sophie at the top of these receipts, doesn't it? And you do sell books, as anyone can see."

"Well, I try to sell books. Sometimes I do; very often I don't."

I was finding this frustrating. "Look, did Abby buy things from you, things that were valuable? Things that would be worth a lot to her partner Rachel? Because everything is going to go to Abby's brother otherwise. Rachel isn't family; she can't inherit Abby's estate in Belgium."

"Shall we start over?" the woman asked when I ran out of steam. She got up and went to the street door, locked it, and pulled down the Closed sign. "My name is Anja," she said, coming back toward me with her hand stretched out. "And your news is nothing I like to hear."

I saw that there were tears in her eyes.

Anja said they had been acquaintances for about a year, ever since Abby had walked into her shop one rainy day and started talking books. They both had a passion for them, especially the work of the underrecognized women modernists of the early twentieth century.

"But these couldn't have been what Abby bought from you. She had a complete collection. She'd been building it for years."

"You keep assuming that Abby bought from me," said Anja. "And she did, a bit, but just to show that she appreciated what I was doing. She'd been in bookselling, so she knew its difficulties. Mostly," Anja looked down at the papers on the desk, "I bought from her. That's what those receipts mean."

"But the receipts are for the equivalent of hundreds of dollars." I looked around. "I don't mean to be offensive, but you look like you're barely hanging on."

"Women's literature doesn't sell the way one would wish," Anja agreed.

"Then how . . ."

"I was the middleman. I bought on behalf of someone else."

"A library, a private collector?"

"Look," said Anja. "It wasn't quite on the up-and-up—as you say—what we were doing."

I waited.

"You know, I didn't have lunch today," said Anja. "Just forgot about it. I was going to close early anyway and get a bite. Perhaps you'll join me?" said Anja.

She locked the shop behind us and we walked to a place a block or two away. Anja had recovered from the shock of hearing about Abby, and we let the conversation slip to lighter subjects, to Anja taking up karate again after some years respite, and to my friend Eloise, whom she knew. The disloyal thought went through my head that I could see why Abby might come to Amsterdam to see Anja. She didn't have the beauty of Rachel, but she didn't have her dependency either. Not that Abby had ever said in so many words that Rachel was too much for her; the nearest she'd come during a recent visit was to say that both of them had had a hard time adjusting to Belgium, and that Rachel especially seemed lonely.

We ordered sandwiches. I had a coffee, Anja a small glass of Dutch gin, *genever,* and a beer. It had begun to rain, and the afternoon had become dark and drawn-in. The little bar itself was dark too, one of those places the Dutch call the brown cafes. We could have been in the eighteenth century, looking through the small-paned windows onto the canal, the carpeted table between us.

It wasn't until we were settled that Anja began to speak again. "How much do you know about her aunt? The one she inherited from?"

"Almost nothing. One day Abby was living an ordinary life in London, working in a bookstore, scrabbling to make the rent, and the next she was living in Brussels in an expensive flat with no visible means of support."

"Her aunt was named Amanda Lowe. She came over to Europe as a nurse during the last war and married one of her patients, a rich Belgian. This aunt made over her flat to Abby before she died, with the provision that Abby live there and keep it up. But she didn't leave Abby any money. Perhaps she meant to, but died before she could manage it. The money went automatically to Abby's brother."

"A beautiful flat but no money to live there. Is that why Abby was selling off her books and manuscripts?"

"Yes. Although I believe she was trying to work out some agreement with her brother, and he was being difficult. I don't know exactly. We didn't discuss that."

"And meanwhile Abby still had to live," I said and, guessing, "Was there something that her aunt had that was a secret, that was valuable, that could be sold?"

"Exactly."

"But what was it?"

There was another pause, while Anja took a bite of the sandwich in front of her.

"This aunt," she finally said. "Amanda Lowe. Later Madame Leconte. She was an interesting woman. Before she came to Europe and all that, before she was in the war and married this Belgian man, she had led a different life. Almost been another person, so to speak."

"Go on." It was raining harder now, and I could see people scuttling down the street and across the bridge with umbrellas pulled down over their heads like black crows' wings.

"She lived in Greenwich Village for a time. She had some friends, all girls. Girls she had been to college with in the 1920s. I think Amanda fancied herself something of a writer. She wrote stories and reviews in the 1930s for several journals, and she started novels that she didn't finish. They're about love between women. Very interesting. But unfortunately not very good."

"Manuscripts?" I said. "Abby was selling her aunt's manuscripts?"

"Not quite. I'm afraid they would be worth very little, though gay scholars would find them interesting. However there was also some correspondence with several of her past lovers, and that correspondence is worth a great deal, because some of it is with . . ." and here Anja, in a lowered voice, mentioned one of the best known writers of the twentieth century.

"But she's not a . . ."

"Precisely."

We sat in silence for a while. Anja had another beer. I had another coffee. The rain came down.

I finally asked. "Why did you ask immediately if something had happened to Abby."

"Did I?"

"Why should you have thought that something had happened to her?"

"I don't know. You looked so serious I guess. That's all. I thought the worst. Most people think the worst, don't they?"

I thought about this. "The Dutch often do, I've noticed."

Anja smiled, but in something of a strained manner. "Did Rachel send you to Amsterdam to find me?"

"Yes."

Anja nodded. "I thought Abby must have mentioned something, though she said she wanted to keep it all confidential."

I was about to say, Rachel doesn't seem to know anything, but I held my tongue. All of a sudden I didn't know what Rachel had known or hadn't known. I was equally unsure about Anja. Had there been something more between Anja and Abby than it appeared? Had they been lovers?

Anja drank her beer and seemed thoughtful, "It was a sweet tale, wasn't it? Rachel leaving her husband the doctor for Abby, leaving her beautiful home, her friends. Rachel was one of those women who haven't a clue they're lesbian and then suddenly, it hits them and they're completely changed."

I sat listening to Anja tell the story I'd heard before from Abby. How Rachel had come to London with her husband and had stopped at a crowded pub across from the British Museum. How Abby happened to be there too and offered Rachel a chair. How the next thing they knew they were wandering the streets at midnight and fireworks were going off somewhere. I was listening, thinking, and staring absently through the cafe's windows when I imagined that I saw a familiar figure—something in the flicker of cloth beneath a raincoat, the set of the head—slip around the corner opposite us.

But why would Rachel, if it were Rachel, have followed us to this cafe? Why would she have sent me to Amsterdam and then followed me herself?

"A sweet tale," Anja repeated. "But thcy had to live in the real world. It was Rachel who insisted that they move to Brussels. A beautiful flat full of antiques, no rent to pay; it must have seemed ideal compared to their one-bedroom flat in Stoke Newington. But neither of them liked Brussels, and it was Abby who had to figure out how to support Rachel."

The figure was gone. I was sure I'd imagined it. On a dark afternoon, one raincoat looked pretty much like another. I turned my attention back to Anja, who was finishing up with, "She loved Rachel, it wasn't that, but Abby was never a one-woman woman. It didn't suit her. Rachel was jealous. I think Abby may have had someone in London. She was always going over to London to see her."

"And you and Abby . . . ?"

"Oh heavens, no." But Anja blushed.

"Why did she tell you so much?"

For the first time, Anja looked abashed. "I suppose I've been talking too much. The shock and everything."

"She must have trusted you to tell you about her aunt and Rachel and everything," I said. But I thought, with pain now that Abby was dead, Why didn't Abby ever tell me this?

"That's strange," said Anja, when we got back to the shop. "I could swear I locked the door when we left."

For there were two customers inside, browsing around the shelves. Anja gave a quick look at her desk and cash box. Nothing seemed to have been disturbed. Her face returned to its equable expression, and she spoke pleasantly in Dutch to her customers, who answered her in German.

But I remembered the figure in the raincoat outside the brown cafe, and for the first time a little shiver of doubt passed through my mind about Rachel. A hit-and-run outside the Gare Midi. Happens all the time. Who had been running and why?

When I called Rachel in Brussels, she wasn't there, but I left a message that I needed a little more time in Amsterdam and that I would see her tomorrow. I wasn't sure why, but the idea of spending the night in that luxurious flat with Rachel seemed less than appealing.

I went back to the Hotel Virginia. In the dining area, the breakfast tables were pushed to the wall and Joke was practicing some incredible contortions on a mat on the floor.

"Come on down, Cassandra. Let me teach you a few tricks."

Some tricks I'm never too old for, but I didn't think that was what Joke had in mind. Fortunately Eloise wafted in at that moment with a pot of tea and cups on a tray. She looked as benevolent and tousled as she usually did, as if she'd just awoken from a long and particularly pleasant nap, but I knew that she'd been up since five, dealing with breakfasts and check-outs, supervising the cleaning of the rooms, dealing with reservations, shopping, and welcoming new guests.

I asked Eloise if she knew Anja.

"Not well, but yes. I've found absolutely incredible books on her shelves and the prices are reasonable. It's too bad the shop doesn't do better. Recently she told me she might have to close it if things didn't improve."

As we had our tea, I told her, as briefly as I could, about Abby selling her aunt's correspondence, the love letters between Amanda Lowe and the woman who'd won the Pulitzer and had often been mentioned in connection with the Nobel.

"But she's not a . . . well!"

We looked at each other and shook our heads.

"I don't understand this constant preoccupation with who is and who isn't," complained Joke from a position resembling a tangled phone cord. "Who the hell cares?"

"Only literary scholars, dear Joke," said Eloise. "They love to pry open closets. More fodder for dissertations."

For myself, I'd often found it a bittersweet pleasure to read biographies of famous men and women who had spent so much of their life's energy keeping their love affairs with members of the same sex quiet. They were entitled to their privacy, but we who are openly gay also have, if not a right, then a great longing and need not to feel as lonely as we have sometimes.

"But who did Anja sell the papers to, I wonder?" asked Eloise. "A private collector? A university? Some special collection? And why did Abby choose Anja?"

"I imagine she thought going through Anja would be more discreet than using her contacts in London. Anja said what they were doing wasn't on the up and up, but there's nothing illegal about selling manuscripts."

"And so far it's not illegal to out famous people."

"So it must have had something to do with the estate. Abby wasn't supposed to sell anything in the flat perhaps, including old letters."

"I still have academic friends," Eloise. "I'll see what I can find out. I wonder," she stopped as she was getting up and looked at me. "Could there be something more to all this than a hit-and-run?"

"You're not thinking there's something suspicious about Abby's death, are you?"

But Eloise was already out the door. From the floor, Joke said, "I would say that's exactly what Eloise is thinking. And maybe you should be too."

The next morning I took an early train to Brussels, which gave me plenty of time to consider what I'd gotten myself into. Had my friend been murdered by her lover Rachel? Why? And what was Anja's involvement? Why had she assumed that something had happened to Abby? To whom was Anja selling the correspondence, and for how much? What had happened to that money?

I got off at the Gare Midi and had a look around. Although the streets surrounding it were a bit grimy, the station itself had been renovated inside and had plenty of passengers. Someone must have seen something. I went back outside and talked to the taxi drivers. I asked them if they'd heard about the hit-and-run the previous week.

"Oh yes," they remembered it (*"Horrible."*); that is, they'd heard about it; well, none of them had actually witnessed it. But Paul had, and he had an afternoon shift today. If I came back around two or three, I could surely talk with him.

"You're from the insurance, aren't you?" said one cabby wisely, and I didn't dissuade him.

Next I went to the local police station and was shuffled around to various desks until the inspector in charge of the case turned up and led me into his office. I introduced myself this time as an American journalist, which flummoxed him slightly.

"I assure you, Madame," he said, "that we have done everything in our power to locate the driver and the car. But it was twilight, the worst time for identifying anything, and it was raining hard and the license plate was covered with mud." He paused. "This woman was important in America?"

"*Très importante,*" I said, and thought, To her friends.

When I arrived at the apartment off the Avenue Louise around noon, I found Thomas, Abby's older brother, there. In early years Abby had talked about him sarcastically; in later years not much at all. I couldn't remember what he did for a living, only that when they'd been growing up he'd called Abby Butt-Face. And there was something about their father's business being a problem between them. I couldn't recall the details, only that Abby, much like I had, had left home at an early age when it came out she was a lesbian.

He didn't look at all like Abby. He was about fifty and plump, with a bald head fringed with seaweed-black hair and sarcastic furrows on either side of his bitten-in lips.

He hardly acknowledged me as Rachel let me in, but continued circumnavigating the room with a long list that was presumably the inventory from the security box. Occasionally he would bark a question at Rachel, but mostly he ignored her, much as if she'd been the charwoman.

Rachel appeared groggy and anxious at the same time, as if whatever pills she'd taken to sleep had dulled her wits without bringing her rest. She was still in her bathrobe.

"How did it go in Amsterdam?" she asked eagerly, but in a low voice. "Did you find the bookshop? Did you find what Abby might have been buying?"

"A woman called Anja runs it. I had a drink and a chat with her. Did Abby ever mention her?"

"I don't think so."

"But clearly she went to Amsterdam about a half a dozen times over the past year. Didn't you ask her what she was doing there, who she was seeing?"

"I just thought she was restless, just like I was. In Amsterdam she could talk English, feel freer than here."

"But you didn't go with her?"

"No. She . . . didn't want me to come."

"Just like she didn't want you to come to London?"

"No," Rachel whispered.

She looked pretty miserable. But I hardened my heart against her, remembering, the inspector's words, "It was twilight; it was raining. The car had mud on its license plate."

"Where was Abby returning from that night she was at the train station?"

Rachel jumped.

"Or was she going off somewhere?" I continued casually. "She was . . . going to Amsterdam."

"In the evening?"

But Rachel had composed herself. "Why shouldn't she go in the evening? Anyway, you know as well as I do that she kept her life . . ."

"Private?"

"Secret," said Rachel. "I didn't ask. She didn't offer information."

Except to Anja, I thought. Abby seemed to have told Anja everything. Rachel and I had been whispering in a corner of the apartment, and both of us started when Thomas said, "Is this the Louis 16th chair?"

Rachel nodded to him and muttered, "He doesn't have a clue, the greedy philistine."

I said casually, "So did Abby's aunt specify that not only could the flat not be sold, but none of the articles in it? Is that why Abby resorted to selling the correspondence? It probably wasn't listed on any inventory."

"I don't know what you're talking about."

"Did Abby know you couldn't inherit? Obviously *you* didn't."

"Cassandra, I asked you to go to Amsterdam and meet with someone at this Antikvaariat Sophie. And you come back giving me the third degree."

"And that's another thing. Why did you make me go to Amsterdam when you were going there yourself? Did you just want her out of the bookstore so you could get in and look for something?"

Rachel was silent. I took out the envelope still filled with money and handed it back to her. "This is nothing I want to be involved in."

Thomas was wandering near the bookshelves. "Those aren't your aunt's books," Rachel told him sharply, coming over to him. "They were your sister's."

"Everything of my sister's is mine now," he reminded her.

"Well, there's nothing valuable on those shelves."

"I'll be the judge of that."

We watched him scan the titles, pull down a few of the more expensively-bound books, and look at them. He obviously had no idea that a book in worn paper covers, but signed by Virginia Woolf, was many times more valuable than a leather-bound reprint of a Jane Austen novel. I could see myself that Abby's collection was sadly diminished.

Rachel walked back across the room to where I stood near the door. "Insufferable man," she muttered.

"When exactly did he arrive?"

"This morning."

"There's no chance he could have come a few days ago?"

"Why would he have . . ." Rachel stopped and looked at me. "You don't think . . . " A stain of red came surging up from her chest and into her face. "Abby was murdered?"

I wasn't sure how far I wanted to go in this direction with Thomas still in the room, even though we were both whispering. "It's possible."

"Then you think her brother . . . or even I . . . or this woman Anja? But why?"

"Love and money, the two usual motives."

"You think I might have run over the woman I loved and left her lying in the street?"

"If you were jealous enough. Or desperate enough about money."

"Okay, that's enough. Get out. I thought you were a friend; I thought you would help. But now I see you're out to punish me for some reason. You can leave."

"I didn't say it was you," I tried to explain, but she had opened the door and practically pushed me out. "You admit you were jealous of Anja," I said, as the door closed firmly behind me.

I could have gone to the police station with my suspicions, but I hesitated. I didn't have enough facts, and Rachel's expression of total horror showed she really was surprised to find herself accused. I needed to know more. As I made my way back to the train station, I remembered an evening the three of us had spent in London a few years before. We'd dined well and drunk moderately and laughed enormously, and I'd gone away not so much envious as satisfied: Abby was happy with Rachel.

Things could change. Anja said that Abby wasn't a one-woman woman, which to me was a fairly clear indication that they'd been involved. I wondered who the lover in London was. I tried to see it from Abby's perspective, as I sat on a bus travelling through a gray mist that made it seem much later than early afternoon. She had moved to Brussels because of the flat, and in order to satisfy Rachel's desire for a better standard of living than they'd had in London. But neither of them was happy there. They didn't have friends; they didn't have community. Abby began to wander. Rachel was lonely. There were arguments. Each blamed the other. Rachel suspected affairs, and probably she was right.

But then why didn't Abby leave her? Why did she sell off her book collection and try to sell her aunt's letters, if not to continue to stay in Brussels and support Abby?

I tried hard to recall our last conversation. It had been about a month ago, in bleakest January. Abby had been casual, as usual. "Hi, I'm in town. Meet me for a cappuccino at the usual spot, all right?"

As I had walked up Coptic Street, I saw her just emerging from the bookstore where she used to work. I caught up with her there. To my surprise, she'd seemed a little embarrassed. "Just visiting Peter," she hastened to say, as if that wasn't exactly what I would have assumed.

She had seemed very glad to see me, and we'd spent an hour catching up. She wanted to know all about my recent travels, and I amused her with stories of Luisa Montiflores and her boundless ego. Abby and I had rarely talked about anything very important to us except in a slantwise, jocular fashion, but this time, she'd seemed especially anxious to keep the conversation off herself. When I asked how Brussels was, she shrugged. "It's gloomy in winter, but then every place is. We're doing a lot of reading." And then she'd changed the subject. I'd tried to drag it back—"How long do you plan to be there?"—and that was when she'd made her remark about privacy and secrets. It wasn't really any of my business, she let me know.

I got off at the station and asked for the cabby Paul, but he had just taken off with a fare. I went into the Gare Midi and found a bank of phones. First I called London.

"Peter? This is Cassandra Reilly. You may not remember me, but I was a friend of Abby's." I told him, as gently as I could, that she had been killed.

"But I just saw her recently," he said. "Just last month. I can't believe it. Not Abby."

"She worked for you for donkey's years, it seems."

"And I've missed her badly since she left for Brussels. Couldn't understand why she wanted to go there and once there, since she was so unhappy, why she didn't return."

"She told you she was unhappy?"

"Oh well, you know Abby. She never told anyone the total truth, only the version that suited her at the moment. But of course that's what made her such a good book buyer. If someone brought in a load of books, imagining they were valuable—and of course sometimes they would be valuable—Abby would never let on. She knew such a vast amount, but then she would, wouldn't she? Raised in the trade."

"What do you mean?"

"Well of course you knew," Peter sounded surprised. "Her father had Lowe's Antiquarian Bookstore, that excellent shop on the West Side in Manhattan. People still remember it—the marvelous selection, the old wooden shelves up to the ceiling, the books in the glass cabinets, beautiful books. Abby grew up in the shop. But when her father died suddenly, her brother was the one to take it over. I don't know the reason why. I suppose because he was the boy and she was still too young."

I was remembering a very early conversation with Abby. "The business went to my brother, even though he didn't love it. He was just greedy and thought it would make him rich. But he doesn't know anything." But I had not remembered that it was a bookstore. Perhaps she hadn't told me.

"You don't have to answer this if you don't want to," I said. "But is there any possibility that she was selling you titles from her collection?"

"I'm afraid so, yes," he said. "I hated to see her do it, but she said she couldn't really manage otherwise. She said

178

she hoped that something was going to come through soon though."

I thanked him, hung up, and called Anja.

"I've been thinking about our conversation," I told her. "And it's occurred to me to ask which university you were selling the letters to."

"I'm afraid I can't really tell you that."

"But Abby is dead now. Whatever agreement you made with her can't be valid. Is the sale still in progress? Did you receive the money? How much was it and what happened to it?"

"It's not that I don't want to tell you, Cassandra," she said a little nervously. "But I'd prefer to wait a little. Things *are* still in progress with the university, and I'd rather not queer the negotiations, so to speak. Besides, it's a little unclear to me at the moment what right you have exactly to ask all these questions. If you're working with Rachel, I must say that I have some reservations."

She had put it very diplomatically, but I understood that she was not going to tell me much more. Perhaps she was regretting that she'd revealed me so much already.

"You suspect Rachel?" I finally said.

"Just ask her what she took from my desk yesterday. See what she says," said Anja and rang off.

As I walked past the ticket office, I had the strong urge just to get on the first train back to London. I could sleep on the ferry from Ostend. I was sick of this whole business and not sure why I was getting more deeply involved. But I kept walking and when I got back to the taxi stand, Paul was there.

Fifteen minutes later I was back on a bus going in the direction of the Avenue Louise. I hadn't found out much from the cabby, but I'd found out a few things. Paul was from the former Yugoslavia and didn't speak much French. He hadn't given me the clear answer that I wished.

"A gray Fiat, very hard to see," he said. "New one, not old. Very much mud on the license plate."

"But how could the mud stay stuck?" I asked. "It was raining."

"Brown mud," he said.

"You're sure it was a gray Fiat?" I was not sure if Rachel and Abby owned a car, but I supposed Rachel could have rented one. "Did you see the license plate? Was it from Brussels?"

"Too much mud," he said.

Thomas was gone when I buzzed Rachel from downstairs. She let me in, and seemed subdued. "I didn't expect to see you again."

Somehow she had pulled herself together, had combed her hair and put on a sweater and pants. She had been crying.

She gestured me to a chair and went to make tea. Now that I was getting more familiar with the apartment, I could see that it was not as posh as I'd first imagined. There were definitely antiques, but the wallpaper was spotted and old, the carpets stained. It had a kind of musty smell, too, which probably came from the velvet, slightly moth-eaten drapes.

"I called Peter at Abby's old bookshop," I said when Rachel came back. "He told me that Abby was selling off her collection."

"I could have told you that. We were desperately poor. Abby's books were the only thing of value."

"Why didn't you tell me?"

"I didn't think it was important. The books were sold; the money was used up. What I was trying to find out was how Abby had used the money, whether she had bought anything valuable that wouldn't be in the inventory."

"She didn't buy anything. She sold something to this woman at the Antikvaariat Sophie."

Rachel nodded. "You mentioned some correspondence. As if I knew about it. I didn't, actually."

I explained what it was.

Rachel thought for a moment and then said, "I guess I'm not surprised that Abby didn't tell me about the letters. She probably knew that I wouldn't approve of making money off a youthful love affair. I believe that people should come out when they're ready. Which means that some people are never going to come out, if they can help it."

She went on, "Look, I know that Abby always liked to put it about that she bowled me over and that I left my husband for her. And that's partly true. He gave me an ultimatum and I had to accept it. He'd accommodated himself to my other women lovers, but Abby was more threatening."

"Other lovers?"

"My husband knew I'd experimented, as he called it. In fact, I'd been sleeping with women a long time before I met Abby. But it's true that Abby meant enough to me to leave the life I'd had. It wasn't easy. I didn't have a work permit in London, so I was reduced to doing under-the-table freelance editing, while I waited to get legal status there."

"You were an editor?"

"I'd done editing in New York, yes."

I bit my lip. I had gotten the impression early on that Rachel had had no skills, that Abby had had to support her.

"Then her aunt died. Abby raved about the apartment, said that Brussels was a fascinating city, that it would be a great base to explore Europe from. You know how impetuous and persuasive she could be. I was reluctant. After all, I was finally starting to feel at home in London after five years. But I said yes. It was only when I got here that Abby told me that we had to live in the flat and not sell anything in it. She was trying to work something out with her brother. Meanwhile, we sat here driving each other slowly crazy."

She had used that phrase about Thomas before. "What exactly was she trying to work out?"

"Well, I don't know exactly," Rachel stumbled. "I understood that he got some money from the estate. I don't know how much. But perhaps she was hoping to work out an agreement with him about some of the valuables here. Perhaps that she could give them to him in exchange for cash.

Or that she could sell them and he would take half. I don't know."

"Do you have his address here?"

"Just the hotel name."

"I'd like to ask him some questions."

Rachel shuddered. "It was so creepy, him crawling around looking at everything. He told me that I'd have to be out of here by the end of the week. I hardly know where I'm going to go. Probably back to London. I don't really know anyone here."

"It must have been lonely," I said.

"Abby and I handled it differently. I started learning French, and reading a lot and visiting the museums and the churches. It was really harder for Abby. She hated to think she'd made a mistake in all this. She didn't want to talk about it. But every once in a while she would just get on the train and leave. I figured out what she was doing with her books at some point, that that was why she was going to London. But then she started going to Amsterdam all the time. That I couldn't quite understand."

"But you thought she was having an affair?"

"Was she? With this woman Anja?"

"I don't know, honestly."

"But you think so."

"Yes, perhaps."

"I think so too."

"Is that why you followed me to Amsterdam yesterday?"

"I still don't know how you know that," said Rachel, slowly. "But yes, I did. After you left, I suddenly felt quite wild and had to do something. I took your same train, and followed you to the shop. I saw you talking with Anja. I saw you both leave for the cafe."

"You broke in then. What were you looking for?"

"Some letter, some sign."

"Anja said you took something off her desk."

"I did. It was a note from Abby to Anja."

"Can I see it?"

She went over to the secretary and fetched it. It was short, typed letter.

Dear Anja,
   "No, I don't want to talk on the phone. I'd rather see you. The usual place, on Tuesday evening."

"The usual place—was that in Amsterdam or here?"
"Tuesday was the day Abby was killed," said Rachel slowly. "On her way to the train station."

It was late afternoon when I arrived back in Amsterdam, a day much like the day before, only darker and wetter. I called Eloise from the Central Station.

Eloise had talked with friends in the States. It was true. A buzz had gone around for years that this particular famous woman novelist, who had reached her seventies denying every innuendo, had had lesbian relationships in her youth. But there had never been any proof, and certainly nothing written. There still wasn't.

"Maybe this woman killed Abby," Eloise said.

"It's not *that* much of a stigma."

"Well, maybe to her it is."

"I think I need to talk to Anja again."

"The shop will be closed now. Do you want her address? I went to a party once at her house. It's right near the shop, also on Keizersgracht."

I thanked her and hung up, and made my way by tram and foot to the shop, just to check. The CLOSED sign hung in the window. I walked back across the canal to a cafe and sagged into a chair inside. I was suddenly aware of just how exhausted I was from my back-and-forth trip to Brussels in one day. I hadn't eaten lunch. Hadn't really found out much either. I'd tried calling Thomas at the hotel, but there was no answer. I asked when he had checked in and they told me just the night before. I asked, as casually as I could, if he was out in his gray Fiat and was told, politely but firmly, that

Monsieur had no car. I don't know if I really suspected him. Other than an apartment-full of moldering antiques, what could be in it for him? Still I wanted to talk with him. I could imagine Abby selling first her books, and then the correspondence, to get money. I could imagine her dealing with Anja. I could imagine Anja dealing with a collector or university. I could even believe, though it was difficult, that Rachel knew nothing about this. But I could not imagine why Abby had had to die.

Perhaps I was just making up a big story about the whole thing. Perhaps it was my way of not facing the fact that Abby had been careless, had not been looking, and had died for no reason at all in a hit-and-run accident.

Accidents happen all the time. I ordered a sandwich, and while I waited, I stared out the steamy window at the passing cars. In central Amsterdam there weren't many cars, but they still drove as if they were larger and more important than anything around. It was twilight; it was raining, exactly the same conditions that had existed a few days before at the Gare Midi. I could barely see anything; would not, in fact, have seen the car stop and park in front of the Antikvaariat Sophie if the person who got out had not been wearing complete white. In the gloom she shone.

I threw some guilders on the table and dashed out the door. The white figure had gone inside the store, but no light was turned on. It couldn't be Anja, for she had told me that she walked everywhere. "It's such a problem having a car in the city."

There was no movement in the shop. Could it be Rachel? I crept along the bridge. It was a gray Fiat, the same make of car that had killed Abby. Should I knock on the shop door? Should I write down the license plate? Call the police? Tell them what?

But as I moved up the street toward the shop, I saw something that made me duck quickly into a doorway. It was Anja, getting into the driver's seat of the Fiat. She was wearing a white karate costume, with a brown or black belt. She had something in her hand, a bag. I pressed myself in the doorway as she drove past, and tried to see whether there were streaks of mud on the license plate, but it was too dark. She was going in the opposite direction of the address Eloise had given me for her flat. Probably to her karate class.

I called Eloise back to ask what to do, but she had gone out. Joke answered instead.

"Do you still have your motorscooter?" I asked.

"Yes."

"Can you be at this address on the Keizersgracht in ten minutes?"

"Sure. But why?"

"Because we have about an hour, maybe a little more, to break into someone's house."

It was nothing, Joke assured me, to scramble up a back wall and get inside Anja's flat. "If it had been the front, that would have been harder. But here there are drainpipes and balconies. I'll manage."

We had forced our way through a broken door into the back yard of the tall house. My heart was beating and my mind was racing the clock. I didn't want neighbors to call the police before we'd found any evidence, and I certainly didn't want Anja to come back while we were still there.

"Go back to the front door," Joke told me. "And wait for me to open up. Don't watch me climb," she warned. "You'll probably feel faint."

I did watch her for a moment, just enough to feel faint, and then went round to the front. In less than five minutes, though it seemed like hours, she let me in, and raced back up the two tall flights of stairs to Anja's flat. I followed more slowly, huffing a little.

That's why Joke found the letters first. Not the ones we'd expected. But two little stacks on top of a cluttered desk, as if someone had recently been looking at them.

The first pile Joke handed me were dated in order, starting from about two months before. They were typed, using the same typewriter and paper as the letter Rachel had removed from Anja's desk.

Dear Anja,
Here is a sample letter as agreed. Please let me know what the university says. You know how awkward I feel about selling my aunt's correspondence, but I don't see any other way out at the moment. We are so broke.
Abby

*

Dear Anja,
I'm pleased that the university wants to take the collection, but it doesn't seem as if the price they're offering is really fair. After all the letters do shed a really important light on one of the major writers of our time. Can you try again, either with them or someone else?
Abby

*

Dear Anja,
Thanks for managing to push the price up! It's still not quite what I could wish, but it's quite decent and we're in desperate straits. Any chance of an advance from you on this?
Abby

*

Dear Anja,
Thanks so much for the cash. This should tide us over until the beginning of the month. I don't want to send the letters, so I'll be coming to Amsterdam this weekend to deliver them to you. See you then.
Abby

*

Dear Anja,
Thanks for the second installment. Much appreciated. I'll look forward to the last—and biggest—installment soon!
Abby

*

Dear Anja,

I had the most extraordinary note today, from the letter-writer herself. It was addressed to my aunt and begged her please not to go along with this extortion. What does this mean?

We need to talk!

Abby

There was nothing in these notes to indicate that Anja and Abby were lovers. There was, unfortunately, something to indicate that Anja had not been selling the letters to a university collection at all. A suspicion that was confirmed by two letters with U.S. stamps.

These were typed, with a very black, decisive ribbon, and the tone was firm, but the signature at the end looked old and ill, not bold at all.

Dear Miss de Joost,

You are correct. The copy of the letter you sent from me to Amanda Lowe is indeed legitimate—it would be foolish to pretend otherwise. It was the product of an unwise passion between two college girls and as such, should be relegated to the trash bin. However, as I think it is unlikely you—or the party you say you are acting for (can she really still be alive after all these years? I know I am, but I feel it is much too old)—would be willing to throw it away, I am prepared to pay for this letter and any others you may have.

*

Dear Miss de Joost,

I really cannot abide greed. What seemed to be a simple transaction, a simple and quick erasure of the past, has now turned nasty. I cannot pay the price you name. And I do not like the hint that if I do not come up with the full, exorbitant amount, you will "take your business elsewhere," as you so delicately put it. Take it elsewhere and go to hell. I would rather be outed, than made a damn fool of.

187

I rustled throughout the other papers on the desk. "Is that all, just the two letters from her? Maybe Anja never sold the collection at all. But how strange. She went right to *her.* "

"Maybe she thought she could get more money from her."

"But clearly Abby had no idea of what was going on. She thought Anja was going to—had, in fact—sold the letters to some university."

"Until the writer sent Abby a note telling her about what one might perhaps call blackmailing."

"So Abby had received just a couple of cash advances from Anja. Those were the receipts. But Anja had the letters. She could get whatever price she wanted, either from the writer herself or from other universities."

"Abby must have been on her way to Amsterdam to confront Anja, when . . ."

"But the letters between Amanda Lowe and the writer must be somewhere around here then," said Joke, rustling around in the drawers of the desk.

"What are you doing in my flat?" said a voice from the doorway. She was in her white karate uniform and the belt around her solid waist was black. "What are you doing in my desk?"

I tried to take the defensive. "There's a lot that you haven't told me, Anja." I held up the letter from Abby and the writer. Behind me I could sense Joke moving away in the direction of the window. It was fine for the Human Pretzel to think about clambering down three stories, but I knew that my only way out was the door.

"It's not what you probably think," she said. "I'm not a blackmailer. Abby wanted more money, and so I tried to raise the price. The next thing I know the writer is yelling about extortion."

"But why did you write to her in the first place, not a university special collections or a library?" I was covering for Joke, hoping she could get to the window and out while I distracted Anja. It was clear to me now that she not only had the means—the gray Fiat she had never mentioned—but the motive. She had deceived Abby; Abby had found out; she had decided to kill Abby.

Anja came closer to us and the desk. "I know it looks awful. But you must believe me that I didn't expect things to turn out the way they did. I didn't expect Abby to be killed. I was going to explain it all to her on Tuesday when we met."

"So she was coming to Amsterdam to meet you?"

"Yes. But I got so worked up by the whole thing that I decided to drive there and see if I could catch her at the train station . . ."

"You caught her all right," I couldn't help saying angrily. Joke chose that moment to jump out the window.

"Where's she going?" cried Anja, rushing toward me. "She'll be hurt."

"She can take care of herself," I said. "As for where she's going—to the police I imagine."

"The police! But I didn't do anything to Abby. She was already dead when I got to the Gare Midi." Instead of coming back into the room, Anja began to climb out the window herself. I didn't know what to do. Out of the corner of my eye, I suddenly saw a bundle of old letters, tied with a faded ribbon, that had fallen off the side of the desk.

"All right," I said, in as calm a voice I could manage. "Let's just say I believe you. Would you come back in and explain? If you haven't done anything wrong, you don't have anything to fear from the police."

Slowly she returned to where I was standing, and said, "But that's the trouble, when you do one thing wrong, it makes it look as if you're capable of anything."

I perched on the desk chair and motioned for Anja to sit down, where she wouldn't have a view of the fallen packet of letters.

"It started when Abby found the letters in a box in the apartment," Anja said. "I remember how excited she was when she came to me to tell me who they were from. 'They're worth a fortune to scholars,' she said. And then Abby asked me if I'd help her sell them."

"Why? Why didn't she do it herself?"

"Because of her brother. That's when I heard the whole story about the inheritance and how Abby wasn't supposed to sell anything from the apartment. She was afraid, if her brother knew she'd sold them, he'd either want all or part of the money, or else he would try to use that to get her out of the apartment."

Anja sighed. "I told her I really hadn't done anything like that before and wasn't sure I felt comfortable. But she said she'd tell me who to contact."

"Why didn't you?"

Anja shook her head. "I read the letters, and they seemed so . . . personal. And I knew the writer was still alive. It seemed a really awful thing to do to her. Not to say she's a lesbian of course, but to do it behind her back. So I thought, Well, why not give her the opportunity to buy the letters herself? I truly wasn't thinking of it as blackmail. I just wrote her and sent her a copy of one of the letters and said I had all of them. I only asked whether it was legitimate. I did not name a price at first until I checked with Abby; she told me what to ask. That's when the writer got so angry and accused me of blackmail, and then she wrote a letter to the old address she had for Amanda Lowe and begged her not to go along with this. That's the letter Abby got."

We could hear feet coming up the stairs. Heavy feet. Probably police feet. All of a sudden I was no longer sure that Anja had killed Abby. I thought it was a shame in fact, that the last thing Joke heard before she dove out the window was that Anja had driven her Fiat to the Gare Midi.

There was a powerful knock on the door, and I rose to let them in. I wanted to tell them, "I don't really think she did it," but caution stopped my protest as they handcuffed her to take away for questioning.

The next morning found me again on a very early train to Brussels, this time with the letters in my bag. I read them, one by one, all the way through the Low Countries, and then I read them again. They were beautiful and true, the words of a twenty-year-old in love with a woman for the first time. Why and when had had she become ashamed of that part of her life? Who had made her feel ashamed?

In my case it was my mother; in Abby's case her father. We had both been around the same age—sixteen. We'd both laughed about it afterward, years after we had left home and weren't speaking to our relatives. We had been two tough girls, Abby and I, talking about first loves with a knowing look. Never talking about the shame, the anger, and the hurt of it.

When I arrived in Brussels, it was still only nine. I should be getting a discount from the railway for all the trips I'd taken. I took a cab to the Avenue Louise and woke up Rachel. I knew that Thomas was coming at eleven to make another inspection of the apartment, and I wanted Rachel to delay him as long as possible. Then I went to the post office, where I made a few phone calls to New York. Within an hour, I knew more than I needed. I headed for his hotel.

He wasn't a neat man, the chambermaid told me. She gestured in disgust at clothes dropped anywhere, at the crumbs from his breakfast croissant all over the sheets, and at the papers and letters flung around on the dressing table. I had pressed a franc note into her hands and told her I was his secretary, here to pick up some papers for his meeting today that he'd forgotten. We commiserated over his messiness; then I started searching. After only a few minutes, I found what I was looking for. It corroborated what a bookseller friend in New York had found out for me, that Lowe's Antiquarian Bookshop, while still alive, was in grave trouble.

Here on the desk was a letter from Abby to her brother, offering to trade the apartment in Brussels, with its many fabulous and valuable antiques, for ownership of Lowe's.

"I know that it's not an equal exchange," she'd written. "Our aunt's things are worth far more than the store, especially since you've run it into the ground, but I still have a sentimental attachment to it. I'd be willing to trade fair and square. As for inventory, I have my own collection, and my connections, and I have a deal coming up that I expect to bring in quite a bit."

Oh Abby, Abby, I thought. Why did you brag to him? Why did you tell him the apartment had valuable antiques? Why did you hint at a deal?

I had not cried for Abby when I heard the news of her death, or when I was at the apartment with Rachel or when I stood outside the Gare Midi and looked at the spot where it had happened. But sitting in Thomas's hotel room, on a bed still scattered with croissant flakes, I cried as I read Abby's letter. I cried because that was how I had remembered her and loved her: as a dreamer, a liar, a deal-maker, a sentimental girl with a tough and impish face.

I suppose my story should turn now to how I managed to get the police in Brussels to investigate the possibility that Thomas had indeed killed his sister. How they discovered that he had come into Brussels on Tuesday morning, and had rented a gray Fiat. How they found traces of Abby's blood on the fender of the car, and his fingerprints all over the place. But I find that the subject saddens me. I'm glad he was caught and punished, of course, but his imprisonment will never bring back Abby to me.

As for the rest of us—Anja, quite chastened after a night in jail, went back quietly to doing what she did best, selling books. I sometimes stop there when I pass through Amsterdam, and I come away with books I never meant to buy on subjects that are suddenly fascinating.

After Thomas's conviction, Rachel could have fought to keep the flat, for there were no other relatives. Instead, the Belgian state took it. Rachel said she didn't care; she was just relieved to be out of there. She came with me to Amsterdam for a visit instead, and in the way of many people who come to Amsterdam, she simply stayed. Abby was her true love, but she will probably go happily into old age running the Hotel Virginia with Eloise.

As for the famous letters themselves, Eloise took it upon herself to return them to the woman who wrote them so long ago. "Once," Eloise said, "I would have seen this as an opportunity to make my name. I would have edited the letters and published them without her permission. Not any more. I guess I've completely lost my ambition."

But some time later a letter came in the mail from the famous writer.

> Dear Eloise,
>   Yes, I have burnt them, as you feared I might. I had become brave during the extortion attempt, and then I lost that bravery, as I have lost it before. Perhaps other letters will be found (I was prolific then). It's hard to keep secrets in this life, much less beyond. Though of course by then I will not care. I did read the letters—once—before I burned them. Amanda was a dear friend of mine once. It all came back to me. It wasn't love, not in that way, but it was love no less. Save or burn *this* letter as you will.

The other day, back in London, I walked down Coptic Street, on a light, cool, spring evening. Birds sang—where do those birds live, who live on Coptic Street? There was the smell of lilac wafting on a breeze—where could those lilac bushes grow, in the midst of the city? For a minute or two, I was many years younger, going to meet my lover Abby. I could almost see her running toward me from the other direction, heedless of traffic, running quick and joyous without looking at anything but me.

Mi Novelista

Everyone wants to be a writer, I've found. Everyone thinks it couldn't be that hard. If you spend a lot of time around writers, as I do, the idea becomes even more plausible. They're not really that smart, some of them. They're not really that talented, some of them. All that separates us from them is a book, and sometimes not even that.

I'm a translator, from Spanish to English, which means that although I don't often get credit for, say, the last Gloria de los Angeles novel you picked up, the words in the novel are in fact my words. My English words. My choices. I wrote *crimson,* when I could have written *blood red.* In many cases, I'll tell you modestly, I've improved the words I was given. Texts are fluid. Words can be substituted, each brick of the house removed and replaced. Afterwards, is it still the same house? The original author thinks so. But I know differently.

If what a writer writes is words, then I am a writer. I have books full of my words. But I am not a writer. Not a real one. I used to think I might be. I used to mull over how I might start, used to wonder how to cross the bridge from nobody to novelist. What separated me from them?

Plot and character? When you've translated as many books as I have, it's not hard to look at the creakiness of some story lines, the thinness of most characterizations and to think, "I could do better than that. At least I couldn't do worse." I didn't have much to say as a writer, but again, neither do lots of authors with books on the bestseller list.

They have intriguing lives, or beautiful faces, or strange little gimmicks, but very few interesting ideas. I'd be in good company.

If I could only get started, get my foot in the door. Because I knew, from spending years in the publishing world, that it's easier to write badly *after* you've made a name for yourself. I didn't want to demoralize myself by writing a novel under my own name and then having it rejected. Writers, along with other artists, go through that humiliation all the time. But I didn't want to bother, if that was to be the outcome. I only wanted the good parts: Fame, money, adulation.

And so, innocently, and in the spirit of good fun, I came up one day with the idea of pretending to translate the work of a Latin American woman writer who did not exist.

I chose that continent because I know the literary landscape of South America better than I know that of Spain. The literary landscape I know best is that of Uruguay, but for that reason alone I knew I couldn't make my author Uruguayan. For society outside Montevideo is composed mainly of cattle ranchers, and society inside Montevideo is composed entirely of people who know each other. I couldn't make my author someone in exile either, because those writers are even more visible, and Luisa Montiflores, the brilliant egomaniac whose work I had translated for years, knew them all.

So I decided my novelist, *mi novelista,* must come straight from the teeming urban jungle of Buenos Aires. I hadn't been to the capital of Argentina in some time, but that didn't worry me as I didn't actually plan to set my novel in any place as recognizable as Buenos Aires. I'd read my Italo Calvino and Borges. I'd translated my Luisa Montiflores. I too could create an imaginary city bearing only a tangential relationship to one described in a guidebook.

I called my novelist Elvira Montalban, and one rainy evening in London (where finances had forced me once again to depend on the hospitality of Nicola Gibbons. If you could call a woman hospitable who no longer allowed dairy products in her refrigerator and who practiced the bassoon day and night), I set to work.

My tone, from the beginning, was an intriguing combination of magic realism and some science fiction stories I'd read as an adolescent in Kalamazoo, Michigan. There were no aliens and no spaceships, but the time was the future and the landscape, though not post-nuclear, had been altered through climatic change. A soft blanket of snow lay over everything that had once been equatorial and, in the far north, the glaciers had begun again their slow advance.

Social relationships, too, had undergone a change (unaccounted-for, but that's what's useful about speculative fiction). There was no gender, for instance, and no hierarchy. This was less utopian on my part than the simple desire to see what was left, to see what still divided people. My society seemed to divide between those who were naturally melancholic, which was the preferred state, and those whose cheerful, positive temperaments had to be toned down and reconfigured. Through seminars on the history of sadness, through forced incarcerations in the melancholic institutions, and in some desperate cases, through constant medication or genetic alteration. The title of the book was, in its English translation, *The Academy of Melancholy,* and it contained the intertwined stories of a group of young people and their professors at one of the great schools for sadness in the country.

When I was finished with the first two chapters, I sent them to an editor at the small, rather snooty London house of Farquharson and Pendergast. I could have tried the larger house that published all Gloria de los Angeles's bestsellers, where my friend Simon was an editor. But I was still a bit nervous. I feared that Simon would see through me. Farquharson and Pendergast were very literary, very intellectual, and most important, very well-off.

Jane Farquharson rang only a few days later. She told me she found the "atmosphere" of *The Academy of Melancholy,* the novel I had supposedly translated, rather promising and she asked to see more. She was only critical of the actual translation, which, she said kindly, still read a little like the original Spanish. She wanted Pendergast to take a look, and perhaps another consultant who could read the original and compare them.

"I'm afraid that won't be possible," I said, as crisply as I could.

"Why not? It's been published in Argentina, hasn't it? Or Spain?"

"Not yet."

"Then you must have her manuscript."

"She's a very mistrustful person," I invented. "Actually, completely paranoid. She's so afraid of someone stealing her ideas that she only has the one manuscript. She won't let it out of her sight. I have to sit in her study to translate it. She watches me like a hawk."

There was a pause while Jane took this in, but the secrecy seemed to excite her. I sensed this in her voice when she said, "But where does she live? Here in London?"

"Of course not," I said. "She's in . . ."

"Buenos Aires?"

"No, no," I paused desperately. "She's in . . . Iceland. Iceland," I repeated more firmly. "That's where all the snow comes in."

"Iceland? How did she get to Iceland? What's she doing there?"

"She's in exile. She's underground. She's incognito. She's . . . I don't know much more than you do," I admitted. "I told you, she's paranoid."

"But you *have* met her?" Jane's voice begged for reassurance.

"Of course. Someone passed her name on to me, and I followed it up. Knocked on her door in Reykjavík and persuaded her to let me in. She left Argentina years ago because of the military. Married an Icelandic man, changed her name. Montalban is a pen name, of course."

"I thought you didn't know anything about her."

"These are the barest facts! I don't know anything important. It's a miracle I even got her to show me her work."

"Well . . . "

"If you're not interested, that's fine. I usually work with Simon Gull-Smyth at Penguin. I thought I'd try you first because of your reputation for literary discoveries, but . . ."

She wanted badly to believe me, and so she did. With Pendergast's agreement we soon had two contracts, one for me and one for Elvira Montalban, aka Elvira Antoniosdóttir. The delivery date for the translation was set for March 1, so it could make a fall publication and I received a gratifyingly large advance, the majority of which I promised to pass on to Elvira when I saw her.

"You'll be going to Iceland of course," said Jane Farquharson. "Do give me your address and so on there, so we can stay in touch."

And here I had thought that I was going to be spending the first part of the year in my cozy attic room in Nicola's house. I had already spent some of the advance on buying a comfortable new chair and an elegant desk that I'd been admiring for some time in an antique shop.

"You're going where?" Nicola demanded when I came home that day and began pulling out suitcases in a fit of irritation.

"Bloody Iceland!"

"But Cassandra, it's January."

"Don't you think I know that?"

I'd been to Iceland once, some years ago, in the summer, and it hadn't been too warm and cheerful then either. I called my one acquaintance in Reykjavík, Birgit Birgitsdóttir, the volcano expert, and found that she was just heading off for an island in the South Pacific, where something was rumored to be about to blow, *rumor* being the operative word for getting her out of Iceland during the darkest time of the year.

Birgit was happy to lend me her flat for a month or so, and didn't ask many questions. My flurried explanation about needing complete and utter solitude to finish a project may not have sounded too convincing, but my tone of desperation did.

"I'm just happy you caught me before my flight to Sydney," she said. "Please make yourself at home. There is plenty of whale meat in the freezer."

It was a dark January day when I closed the door on my cozy room, took the tube to Heathrow, and boarded a flight to Reykjavík.

The interior of Iceland is closed to traffic and most travel in winter. What's left, what's open, is the perimeter of the island, which may be imagined as the white rim of frost around a frozen daiquiri. Iceland is as large as England, but the population is only 250,000, and more than half of those people live in Reykjavík, which tends to give the city a huddled feeling.

If I had to be in Iceland in January, I was glad enough to be huddled. I had no desire to travel to the interior.

Of course I went through my advance from Farquharson and Pendergast very quickly. Iceland is the most expensive place in Scandinavia, which is not known for its budget travel. The only cheap thing in Reykjavík is the hot water, which comes from geothermal energy. There is so much hot water, in fact, that when you turn on the tap, you have to wait for the water to get cold.

What did I spend money on? I'm not really sure. I had Birgit Birgitsdóttir's little flat and a whole load of whale meat in the freezer, and hot water whenever I felt like it. Still, it cost me far more to stay in Reykjavík for a month working on my supposed translation than it would have cost me to live in London for six months while pretending to be in Reykjavík.

The idea of making the book about melancholy was a good one, for the long northern nights and the extreme cold acted to give my book a strong quality of gloom that it had not possessed when I had blithely begun it back in London the previous fall. At that point, melancholy had been more a literary *concept* than a state of mind, or actual climatic condition.

In reality, the act of showing two chapters to Jane Farquharson had been an act of bravado. As a translator I'd been accustomed to working with a text, in either manuscript or book form. Now every morning that January in Reykjavík I woke up to a blank page and wondered how to fill it.

I had models certainly, especially the two women writers from South America I'd been translating for years. I could pretend I was the famous magic realist Gloria de los Angeles, whose erotic scenes and little dramas of arrivals and departures often substituted for any real narrative development. I also had the Uruguayan Luisa Montiflores as an example. Her imagination was metaphoric, not anecdotal. Images piled on images. Similes begetting similes. Irony, puns, repetitions, and contradictions. Asides to the reader. Asides to herself. Connections that twisted through the text like colored wires in a circuit board. Her stories looked a jumble until you began to unpick the blue wires from the red. Many of her sentences had cost me an hour or two to rewrite.

But that's what I had always loved about translation: to touch words and tangle with them. To get closer and closer to what I felt was the meaning. I was sensitive to writers' styles. I had an ability to read the mood of a text and to reproduce it. I was able to write, to *mimic* many styles, from academic and elevated to slangy and streetwise. I could pick up the *feeling* of a style. The meaning I struggled over as I translated had nothing to do with the other half of the writer's art, with shaping or transforming reality. My struggle with meaning was definitional, atmospheric. The meaning had to do with words. It never had to do with my life, my thoughts, my imagination.

Thus, when I began to supposedly translate, which meant to actually write *The Academy of Melancholy*, it was impossible for me to imagine the stories coming out of my life. They could only come out of my imagination. They could only come if I imagined myself to be Elvira Montalban writing her stories in Spanish.

Each morning I would take my cup of very black coffee to the table by the window overlooking a concrete modern apartment building, and I would begin to write in Spanish. Occasionally I would get up, muttering in Spanish, and walk around the room, gesturing and acting out emotions. I wrote by hand, in blue ink on white paper. I pulled my hair back in a bun and wore a dressing gown with shabby silk pajamas underneath. I did this until around noon.

Then I took a long, bewildered walk in the dim, street-lighted, often snowy city of Reykjavík, never quite knowing where I would end up. Sometimes I found myself walking around and around the Torn, the frozen lake in the center. Sometimes I wandered into the Museum of Natural History. I went up and down the pedestrian street looking at Icelandic sweaters. Sometimes I discovered new neighborhoods, a hilly road of bright red and yellow wooden houses. I pretended—or truly felt—that I had been dropped into this winter dark city by accident. I either pretended or saw that the faces around me were blank with misery, colorless and bleak. Onto them I projected a regimented sadness.

Sometimes I stopped for coffee or at a restaurant for a midday meal of potatoes and fish. Sometimes I bought cheese and bread to bring home. When people spoke to me in Icelandic, I sometimes answered in Spanish, though we could have easily spoken English. I purposefully learned little of the language there, and yet the sound of it, ancient and melodic, with occasional sighs and many pauses, filtered in through the two other languages I was working with daily, and added something to the rhythm of what I was writing. I knew that Icelandic, still spoken and written as it was during the time of the medieval sagas, kept itself pure by limiting the number of loan words and taking old Icelandic words and putting them together in some new way.

Thus computer had become, in Icelandic, "numbers-prophetess."

At two or three, when the light was already fading from the sky, turning the snowy streets a heartbreaking gray-blue, I would begin work again, this time in jeans and a sweater, with my frizzy hair every which way, a plate of sandwiches nearby, and my laptop computer screen the same dull blue as the snow.

I looked at what I had written with my translator's eye and understood what Elvira had meant to say, if only she could express herself better, if only she had the wealth of the English language at her disposal. I rearranged her syntax and hunted down the meaning of her sentences. I lengthened them and broke them up. I never changed a word she wrote, and yet I changed everything. I worked long into the evening, and lived in her world and shared her bed, and woke up and began the whole process again.

I had no friends, nor did I make any. (And I haven't heard from Birgit Birgitsdóttir since, though I did leave her plenty of whale meat.) My social life was Elvira, and sometimes I chatted with her in Spanish. Once a neighbor who had a condominium in Torremolinos asked me whom I was talking Spanish with in Birgit's flat.

"Elvira Montalban," I said promptly. "You know, the Argentinean novelist?"

"Yes, I *think* I've heard of her," he said, impressed by my conviction.

But someone else in the building must have told him that I was living there on my own, because the next time I saw him, he avoided me.

Occasionally, I would go to lectures at the Nordic House. One evening I saw that an American researcher would be reporting in English on a study he'd done on S.A.D.—Seasonal Affective Disorder. I went, as usual, in a state of some dishevelment. When I stood up at the end to ask my question, I noticed that my voice was rusty with disuse, and also, that I had a Spanish accent.

"Why do you start from the assumption that S.A.D. is bad?" I demanded. "In some cultures, being depressed is considered the norm and the good."

"What cultures are these?" the researcher asked with interest, but then someone explained to him that I was just some crazy South American woman, and he went on to the next question.

I stared at my nailbitten fingers in surprised shock.

I had become Elvira Montalban.

In February, I returned to London and to Nicola's house, and turned the completed manuscript in to Farquharson and Pendergast. Although Jane still complained that the translation read a bit awkwardly in places, she was generally quite impressed with the story—and even more with the mystery of the whole thing. She had me out to dinner at a little place in Soho and tried to pump me for more information about Elvira, but I kept my head. I didn't even respond to Jane's rather too-friendly embrace at the end of the evening. She was the sort of well-bred English girl I simply couldn't feel comfortable around. Nicola knew her from some charity work and said she was horribly snobbish.

Besides, there was Pendergast, and Nicola said *she* was even worse.

The Academy of Melancholy appeared that autumn and was immediately hailed as a work of great gravity and importance.

"A Metaphorical Descent Into the Abyss of Argentinean Politics," said *The Guardian*. "A beautiful and terrifying evocation of terror and exile," wrote the *Times* reviewer. "The author [cribbing here from the publicity materials], resident in one of the Northern countries, splashes the colors of the tropics across the frozen wastes." "Chilling," said the *Telegraph*. (A partial quote.) And, my favorite, "Brilliantly translated by Cassandra Reilly." Farquharson and Pendergast had gotten a friend of theirs to blurb it. "The most interesting book [besides my own] I have read in the last ten years," wrote Gillian Winterbottom. High praise indeed.

I knew that I would be hearing from Luisa. And I did.

"*Who* is this Elvira Montalban?" she wrote, from her residency at the University of Iowa. "What does it mean, 'resident of a Northern country'? I have never heard of her. Someone here read it and says we have a similar style. I don't think so at all. Who publishes her in Spain or Argentina? What is the Spanish name of this book and where can I get a copy?"

After the reviews, invitations to appear on panels and to attend conferences began to pour in for Elvira. The book was published in America, where it made an even greater stir. More offers poured in, and more hysterical letters from Luisa, demanding to know I was not abandoning her for this new writer. Jane referred all requests for interviews and appearances to me, and I referred them, with great regret, to the trash receptacle.

Elvira's fame would plummet like a stone if it were revealed that she was really an Irish-Catholic girl from Kalamazoo, Michigan.

About nine or ten months after *The Academy of Melancholy* first appeared in England, Jane called me. I had been in and out of London, travelling to see friends and pick up work of course, but also to avoid Luisa, who had made two trips to England specifically to track me down.

"I asked you repeatedly about the rights situation, Cassandra," Jane fumed. "And you said she didn't want to be published in Spain or Argentina.."

"That's absolutely true," I said, prepared to defend my position again. "She's writing under a pen name and she's afraid of repercussions."

"Then how do you account for the fact that the book has just been published in Madrid?"

"Madrid? Impossible!" I sputtered. "Completely impossible. Elvira doesn't . . . I mean, she could never, I mean, she would never *allow* . . ."

"Elvira not only allowed it," Jane snapped. "She's promoting it like crazy. She's not only alive and well, but she's not living in Reykjavik. She's living in Madrid. And her face is all over the literary pages of Spain's newspapers. It's a face that, I'm sure I don't have to remind you, you claimed she refused to have photographed."

"Face? Photograph? It must be a joke. I told you, she's reclusive and practically certifiable."

"Don't toy with me, Cassandra." And Jane rang off.

A short time later, a messenger arrived at my door with an envelope from Jane. It contained a batch of clippings from the Spanish newspapers. The face, long, narrow, with heavily made-up eyes, looked completely unfamiliar. I raced through the reviews and interviews, looking for some clue.

"I always wanted to write," she said in one. "But I never believed that my experiences in Iceland would be any use to me. I thought that to write I would have to write directly about the situation in Buenos Aires, and *that* I thought I could never do."

"What changed your mind?" the reporter asked.

"A conversation I had with a stranger some years ago in a cafe," said the false Elvira. "She seemed so fascinated in my descriptions of the snow and the great sadness of that time in my life, that I tried to see what I could make of it."

The liar, the worse-than-plagiarizer, the *thief*.

She wasn't Elvira Montalban. She was Maria Escobar. I remembered her now.

It had been a chance encounter in a cafe in Paris some years ago. An intriguing but not particularly attractive woman, wearing, although it was spring and getting warmer, a half-length jacket. A jacket of rather soiled sheepskin. When she took it off, her dress was surprisingly chic, but also rather soiled, with permanent stains under the arms. She was between forty and fifty, with dyed black hair in a heavy bun, no earrings or other jewelry. She sat at a table outdoors that afternoon, sheltered from the wind. A familiar place. The waiter seemed to know her, but not to like her particularly. Once or twice when she spoke to him, he ignored her for the second it took to let her know she was unimportant to him, and then, "*Oui, Madame?*" And this, too, seemed familiar. She was not insulted. She seemed to expect it. A foreigner in some way, yet her French was excellent.

She took out a portfolio of papers, and two or three small dictionaries, and began to work. I understood immediately. She was a translator. Back and forth her eyes scanned, and her writing was rhythmic and assured. Occasionally she looked up a word, but for the most part it seemed routine work, and not particularly engaging.

Eventually I struck up a conversation with her, in French that quickly turned to Spanish, that was restrained at first, and then more voluble. I had the sense she had not talked with anyone for a long time, and certainly not about her life. She was from Argentina, had spent a time in prison there and had gotten out with the help of Amnesty International, which had sent her to Denmark. There she had married an Icelandic businessman who had taken her back to his country. She didn't live in Reykjavík any longer. They had divorced; for some years she had lived in Paris. She had some work that was fairly unsatisfying in a multinational corporation translating back and forth from Spanish to English to French. Documents of some sort. I remember how her long fingers, with their unkempt nails, fiddled nervously with the papers. Several times she told me that she had a deadline the next day. And yet she made no move to leave.

Nor did I. The waiter ignored us. We let our conversation roam. I listened a great deal, watched her face. Her lipstick was an old-fashioned shade of burgundy and had flaked dryly at the corners of her mouth. She had a faint mustache. She seemed a woman with her life behind her. "I wanted so much more for myself once," I remember her telling me, and the words floated up in the spring evening air, for twilight had supplanted afternoon.

"What did you want?"

"To write," she said.

"Everybody wants to be a writer," I said. "I've often thought of it myself, being a translator."

"But I really wanted it," she told me.

We kissed when we parted and promised to keep in touch, but I was on my way from Paris to Mozambique to visit a friend, and I lost her card almost immediately.

I had not thought of her again, until I saw her photograph in the newspaper.

The cheek of it. Those stories she told me that day long ago were nothing like what I'd written. Or were they? In truth, I had forgotten the substance of what she'd told me. I only remembered the cafe, the waiter, the scent of spring, the way she tapped the papers under her fingers.

But she wasn't going to get away with this. Jane would make sure I never worked as a translator again in England or America, if I didn't get a handle on this and fast.

I called my local bucket shop and got a flight that same evening for Madrid.

Life in Spain, and especially Madrid, doesn't really get going until around midnight, so even though it was after ten when my friends Sandra and Paloma met me at the airport, they told the taxi driver to head into the center, to the Puerto del Sol. First, for old times' sake, we did the rounds of half a dozen bars. In some we had a *pincho*, a mouthful, and in others a *ración*, a plateful. Squid, octopus, shrimp—all fine with me, though I drew the line at tripe and recognizable parts of pigs. We drank a little red wine at each place and then moved on. Eventually we had dinner, and afterward joined the throngs of Madrileños, jamming the sidewalk cafes and narrow streets. It was a May night, warm but not too hot, and it seemed perfectly normal to be wandering around a large city at three a.m. without a fear in the world. We finished up the evening with a Guinness at an Irish bar Sandra and Paloma had recently discovered.

At four we took a taxi to their modern new apartment building far into the suburbs. Sandra and Paloma had come up in the world. When I first knew them, Sandra was on leave from the University of York, writing her dissertation on Women in Nineteenth-century Madrid, and teaching an English class at the university; and Paloma was a struggling scriptwriter. Now Sandra was a professor here and Paloma worked on a hugely successful television show called *¿Quién sabe dónde?* or *Who Knows Where?*

"It's just a missing person show," Sandra explained, as Paloma popped a tape of a recent show in the VCR, "but somehow it's tapped into the national psyche. Everybody watches it religiously."

"I write the scripts," said Paloma. "I have a lot of fun. Of course it's all supposed to be completely true."

The video showed a distraught mother on the phone to her daughter, pleading with her to come home. Strangely enough, a film crew seemed to be right in the mother's pink-and-blue bedroom with her, as well as in the disco where her daughter was shouting, "I hate you, I'll never come home!" into the receiver.

¿Quién sabe dónde? reminded me of Maria Escobar, the word thief. Who knew where she was, indeed? I'd told Sandra and Paloma I was in Madrid to meet with the author of *La academia de la melancholía*, but I hadn't told them the whole story.

"Yes, that book is very well-known," they told me. "The author seemed to come out of nowhere and is a great success. We have a copy if you'd like to read it."

"Oh just leave it around," I said casually. But as soon as they were in bed, I grabbed it and spent the rest of the night reading *La academia de la melancholía*. The same plot, the same characters, the same mood. Everything the same. Except the words. The Spanish was excellent, beautiful, much better than my original Spanish had been, the Spanish I'd written down those snowy mornings well over a year ago in Reykjavík. How could that be? This was a translation of my work from English. But it read as though it was the original Spanish.

Saturday night we went out on the town again, and Sunday we drove to a small village outside the city to visit Paloma's mother. Paloma might be a high-rolling, chain-smoking TV executive during the week, but on Sundays she wore a plain dress and flat shoes and helped her mother make dinner.

On Monday I called Elvira Montalban's publishing house and requested a meeting with the author. "I'm afraid I can't help you," the receptionist said. "Our authors don't have time to meet with readers."

"But I'm her . . . English translator. I came especially from London to meet her."

"In that case, I'll see what I can do."

She rang back in fifteen minutes to say that Elvira had agreed to meet me the following day for lunch. "She's looking forward to it," the receptionist told me.

The restaurant where Maria-Elvira suggested we meet was a typical mesón, a dimly lit inn with a wood oven, a tile floor, and oak beams. The specialties of such places were offal dishes and a chickpea-chorizo stew, know as *cocido*.

I had plenty of time to study the menu and mull over the predilection of Madrileños for brains and intestines and stomach linings, not to mention pig trotters, ears, and even snouts. Maria-Elvira was late, so late that I thought she wasn't going to show. When she finally appeared, I was amazed at the change in her. She looked elegant and well-dressed, no longer with her hair bundled up and her make-up too thick, no longer wearing clothes that seemed wrong somehow. Her face was still long, her brows still heavy, but her hair was fashionably cut and streaked and her lips were a luscious shade of crimson. She made her way over to my table with determined grace, a woman who had found her role.

"Well," she said in Spanish. "We meet again, my friend." She kissed my cheek lightly, as if we were great pals.

I couldn't help it. I admired her. She looked the part of Elvira Montalban so much better than I ever could, me with my wild Irish hair and freckles, with my working-class fears of making a social faux-pas. Maria-Elvira looked Spanish, she looked intellectual, she looked like a writer.

Stop it! I told myself. Elvira Montalban is your creation. This Maria Escobar is nothing but an opportunist.

I handed her my menu without speaking.

"The *menu del día* is very good here," she said, without looking at the menu. "Unless you prefer tripe or brains."

I shook my head. She gestured confidently to the waiter and gave him our order, two *cocido*s, then turned to me with a slight smile that showed her rather large teeth.

I found that I was almost intimidated by her. In Paris, she'd had the look of a displaced person, marginalized by history and geography. She had spoken softly and timidly to the cafe waiter and had cringed when he turned his back on her. She had seemed to me one of those people in the world who have been hurt rather badly, and in many different ways, so that they do not spring back.

Now she did not shrink. Now she took up space.

"Not many of these old places left," she said conversationally. She took out a pack of cigarettes, offered them to me, and then lit up. She hadn't smoked before, but now she seemed to luxuriate in it. She poured wine from the carafe and took a drink. Then she called the waiter over and ordered a better bottle.

"How long have you been in Madrid?" I asked her grudgingly.

"Oh, about two years, perhaps. I stayed on in Paris for a while, but of course I was really dying there, I see that now. I thought at first I was homesick, so I decided to go back to Buenos Aires. But naturally, once I got there, after twenty years away, I realized that everything had changed and I had no place there anymore. I spent about six unhappy months, and then decided to come to Madrid, and to do what I'd always wanted to do, which was to write. Of course, my stay in Argentina was very useful in that it put me in mind of old familiar places, and especially a kind of mood I wanted for my book."

Cocido is usually served in three courses. The first of these, a rich broth with a little rice, now arrived. I thought, This woman must be a schizophrenic. She's actually convinced herself that she's Elvira Montalban. She sounds like she's giving an interview to a newspaper.

"And you, Cassandra," she said, sipping her broth appreciatively. "What have you been up to? Still travelling as much as ever? You were off to Mozambique then as I recall."

"Oh, yes," I said. "Still travelling. That is, when I'm not writing."

"So you're writing too?" No, she wasn't insane. There was a twinkle in her eye. As if this were all a joke.

"You know perfectly well what I've been writing."

"I don't, really," she answered, dabbing gently at the corners of her mouth. "Is it something based on your experiences, or did you borrow someone else's?"

Just then a couple of men, middle-aged, genial, expensively suited, entered the restaurant. Maria-Elvira waved them over. They all kissed and then she introduced them to me.

"My publisher," she said, "and my editor. This is Cassandra Reilly. She translated my book into English."

"Ah, yes, an unusual case," said the publisher. "It's not often where the translation comes out before the original."

"I'd tried many publishing houses and had been turned down," said Maria-Elvira sweetly. "Without the book's success in England and America, I'm afraid I wouldn't have had a chance in Spain."

"Well, the novel never crossed *my* desk," said the editor. "I'm sure I would have noticed it."

They settled at a table in the corner, out of earshot. The second course of the *cocido* arrived: chickpeas, with the vegetables from the stew, cabbage, leeks, onions, turnips. Maria-Elvira attacked it with relish.

"You set this up, didn't you?" I said. "Suggesting we meet at the restaurant where you know they always eat. It wasn't coincidental."

"I don't believe in coincidence," Maria-Elvira said. "Now where were we? Your writing? Yes. You were telling me where you get your ideas."

"You stole my book," I said. "You're not Elvira Montalban. You're Maria Escobar."

"You stole my life."

"I made the stories up. They're not realistic. They're fantastical."

"You took my stories about my preparatory school and about my teachers, and you turned them into something else. You put the school in the future, and let the snow fall and gave it a fancy name. But it's my life. You captured my life perfectly."

"Living a life is not the same as writing about it," I said, but I faltered slightly.

"That chapter where the girl from the happy family sees her parents dragged off by the militia? That conversation in the interrogation chamber? That clandestine love affair between the powerful professor and the young student? I could name several more, many more scenes that were just as I told you. Didn't I tell you too about my terribly sad marriage to the Icelander and those dreadful winters we passed in Reykjavík, hardly speaking while the snow fell on and on? Didn't I?"

Her voice sounded so familiar to me. As if it were an inner voice of mine made visible. As if the cadences of her speech were something I'd written down from dictation.

The waiter asked me if I'd finished my second course. I'd hardly touched it, though Maria-Elvira had finished hers. He brought the third and final plate: a pile of meat—beef,

213

chorizo, blood sausage, some bits of unidentified organs and, poking out from the middle of the pile, a pig's trotter.

Instead of tackling it immediately, as she had the other two courses, Maria-Elvira brought out a pile of papers from her bag. "You see, I've already been writing my second novel. The publisher has accepted it. It will be published next year."

"You can't do that. You're not Elvira. I'm Elvira."

"Have you written anything more by Elvira Montalban?"

I had to admit that no, I had not.

"Because you have nothing to say. You have no stories to tell, now that you have used up mine. But I still have stories to tell."

I opened my mouth, but stopped. My story was that of an Irish-Catholic girl from Kalamazoo. I had been inventing myself as a traveller and translator since I left home. I had no stories that I wanted to tell, no stories that were either true or literary, no stories I thought anyone would want to hear.

Now Maria-Elvira began to eat, and gestured to me to join her. "I've always found this dish so curious, how it's served. Separating all the parts out, the broth, the vegetables, the meat. It's quite a metaphor, don't you think? My ideas were the broth, nourishing but thin; your translation the vegetables, good but not filling. And my final version is the meat, chewy, spicy, substantial."

"You call it a final version. You don't call it a translation?"

"They were my words to start out with and now they're my words again. You will never write another book, Cassandra Reilly, but I will write a dozen more. I'm a writer now. I don't know how it happened, but it happened."

"I know how it happened," I began, but in truth I didn't know. The process from nobody to novelist was just as mysterious to me as it had ever been.

The editor and publisher came over again. "I was just telling Cassandra about my next book," said Maria-Elvira, patting the manuscript beside her.

"It's quite brilliant from what I've seen," said the editor. "We expect it to have an even greater success than *La academia de la melancholía.*"

"Now all we need is title," said the publisher. "Has anything come to you yet?"

"Yes," said Maria-Elvira. She pushed her plate away. All that was left of the meat course was the bones. "I'm thinking of calling it simply *The Translator.*"

I started.

"Because that's really what it's about, my years of translation."

"*The Translator,*" said the editor. "Plain and yet evocative."

"I like it too," said the publisher, turning to me, "Have you and Elvira already begun the translation process?"

"Yes," said Maria-Elvira quickly. "I wouldn't have anyone else. Because Cassandra understands the craft extremely well. She understands it's not just the art of substituting words for other words. It's a form of writing in itself. What one might call—a collaboration."

Pendergast wasn't pleased of course, but Jane Farquharson took the long view, especially after she received a charming letter from Elvira Montalban explaining the reasons for the secrecy. She told Jane that she would be happy to give her new novel to Farquharson and Pendergast on the condition that I, Cassandra, remain her translator. Along with the letter she sent a box of hothouse flowers.

And that's how I became the translator of, or rather, the collaborator of, Elvira Montalban, the author to whom Luisa Montiflores is often compared these days, the comparison, of course, highly favoring Elvira.

About the Author

BARBARA WILSON, cofounder of Seal Press and publisher at Women in Translation, is author of five mystery novels, two story collections, three literary novels, and a memoir. Her first Cassandra Reilly mystery, *Gaudí Afternoon*, won a Lambda Literary Award and a British Crime Writers Award, and is currently being made into a motion picture. Her mysteries have sold hundreds of thousands of copies in the United States, Germany, England, Japan, Italy, and Finland.

Third Side Press
. . . because every issue has more than two sides.

The book you are holding is the product of work by an independent women's book publishing company. Third Side Press publishes lesbian literary fiction and feminist health books. For a free catalog, contact us at Third Side Press, 2250 W. Farragut, Chicago, IL 60625, 773-271-3029, ThirdSide@aol.com.